"This fabulously fun series is bursting with style, glamour, and tons of heart." —Sarah Mlynowski, bestselling author of *Bras & Broomsticks*

"Violet : onderfully witty and sweetly sensitive. She's not your typical to odel; she's more like your best friend—only prettier."
—Kristen Kemp,
author of *Breakfast at Bloomingdale's*

"A story for any girl who ever wondered what it would be like to have her wildest dream come true."
—*New York Times* bestselling author Sarah Dessen

"A fun, fashion-filled, fast-paced read! Violet is a hero for all of us wallflowers." —Carolyn Mackler, bestselling author of *Guyaholic*

"For every girl who's ever looked at a glossy magazine and wanted to know the story behind the picture. Melissa Walker creates fiction couture—unique and beautiful. On the runway or off, Violet shines."
—Ally Carter, bestselling author of
I'd Tell You I Love You, But Then I'd Have to Kill You

"*Violet on the Runway* is a novel about fashion, but it's also a sensitive portrait of adolescence—simultaneously funny and painful. Walker excels at characterizing those moments we've all experienced, from bumbling in front of the cute boy to being misunderstood by one's parents." —*Nylon*

violet IN private

melissa walker

BERKLEY JAM, NEW YORK

THE BERKLEY PUBLISHING GROUP
Published by the Penguin Group
Penguin Group (USA) Inc.
375 Hudson Street, New York, New York 10014, USA
Penguin Group (Canada), 90 Eglinton Avenue East, Suite 700, Toronto, Ontario M4P 2Y3, Canada
(a division of Pearson Penguin Canada Inc.)
Penguin Books Ltd., 80 Strand, London WC2R 0RL, England
Penguin Group Ireland, 25 St. Stephen's Green, Dublin 2, Ireland (a division of Penguin Books Ltd.)
Penguin Group (Australia), 250 Camberwell Road, Camberwell, Victoria 3124, Australia
(a division of Pearson Australia Group Pty. Ltd.)
Penguin Books India Pvt. Ltd., 11 Community Centre, Panchsheel Park, New Delhi—110 017, India
Penguin Group (NZ), 67 Apollo Drive, Rosedale, North Shore 0632, New Zealand
(a division of Pearson New Zealand Ltd.)
Penguin Books (South Africa) (Pty.) Ltd., 24 Sturdee Avenue, Rosebank, Johannesburg 2196,
South Africa

Penguin Books Ltd., Registered Offices: 80 Strand, London WC2R 0RL, England

This book is an original publication of The Berkley Publishing Group.

This is a work of fiction. Names, characters, places, and incidents either are the product of the author's imagination or are used fictitiously, and any resemblance to actual persons, living or dead, business establishments, events, or locales is entirely coincidental. The publisher does not have any control over and does not assume any responsibility for author or third-party websites or their content.

PRINTING HISTORY
Berkley JAM trade paperback edition / August 2008

Library of Congress Cataloging-in-Publication Data

Walker, Melissa (Melissa Carol), 1977–
     Violet in private / Melissa Walker.—Berkley JAM trade paperback ed.
         p.   cm.
     Summary: Enrolled at Vassar College, Violet Greenfield, an insecure nineteen-year-old supermodel, accepts an internship with "Teen Fashionista" magazine and finds herself falling in love with her best friend, Roger.
     ISBN 978-0-425-22182-2
     [1. Models (Persons)—Fiction. 2. Universities and colleges—Fiction. 3. Self-confidence—Fiction.]
I. Title.

PZ7.W153625Vh 2008
[Fic]—dc22

                                                                              2008012665

PRINTED IN THE UNITED STATES OF AMERICA

10   9   8   7   6   5   4   3   2   1

For my grandmother
Carol Virginia Scanlon Walker,
who showed me how to be kind
and gracious, with an edge.

acknowledgments

Thanks to my agent, Doug Stewart, and my editor, Kate Seaver, for their continued enthusiasm for Violet! Extra points to the art department at Berkley JAM because they've made Violet's world so vividly beautiful on all three covers. Erica Colon, in marketing, and Caitlin Brown, in publicity, you guys are complete rock stars. I'm so grateful for every reader who gets in touch just to say hi—you continue to brighten my days. And for Dave, who makes me feel like I can do anything.

one

"Oomph!" As I pull a yellow jacquard print dress on over my head, my long, thin hair goes totally static. The dress is trying too hard, I realize, bending down awkwardly to survey my six-foot-one frame in the full-length mirror that's been in my room since third grade. And the makeup is over the top. I ditch the dress and grab jeans and an extra-long white tank top. I zip an old black hoodie over it and head to the bathroom to wash off my blue mascara, and I pull my stringy brown hair into a ponytail. Better to be less fashion-y and more *me*.

I hear the Rabbit horn honk three times in quick succession. My best friend Julie has this old VW that she and our other BFF Roger and I have been riding in since the end of tenth grade when Julie got her license. Roger and I used to joke that it was at least two-thirds our car because of the time we spent in it, but Julie still won't let us drive it. She's kind of controlling like that. But whatever, I'm not that good at stick shifts anyway.

I check myself out in the mirror one more time before I run downstairs. Yeah, I look like me. I dab on the Tokyo Plum Blossom gloss that I picked up in Paris last year—just so I can feel a hint of glamour.

What's weird is that I'm spending all this energy thinking about what to wear as I get dressed to go meet *my two best friends in the world*. They're both finally back for winter break and we're heading to Elmo's Diner to catch up. I've spent the last couple of months with basically nothing to do in our hometown of Chapel Hill, North Carolina, and without Roger and Julie around I thought I might go crazy. I've read something like twenty books (though four were mangas, which don't take as long as normal books, I'll admit). I can't wait to see Roger and Julie, but I'm nervous too. Since we said good-bye last summer and they started their freshman years of college in September, a *lot* has happened.

"Vexing Violet!" says Roger in a spot-on imitation of my insane Tryst Models agent, Angela Blythe. "So lovely to see you in your street clothes." I stick out my tongue at him as I slide into the backseat of the Rabbit. His blue eyes are shining behind black-framed glasses, and his jet-black hair is longer, almost touching his shoulders, which seem to have gotten even broader since I saw him a little over a month ago. My heart does a quick flip-flop, but I will myself to act normal—it's just *Roger*. He's wearing a corduroy coat with white wool around the edges. Very seventies.

"Did you pick up that jacket at Andy's Chee-Pees?" I ask, naming an overpriced vintage store in Manhattan that hipster NYU kids like Roger frequent.

"No, Nancy Drew," he says, rolling his eyes. "Street vendor on Tenth. Thirty-five bucks."

"Hello?!" says Julie, leaning over the front seat for a hug. "Do I get some love here or is this the Roger-and-Violet hour?"

"Sorry, Jules," I say, reaching out for a squeeze. "It's so good to see you!" She smiles and sits back in her seat, putting the Rabbit in reverse. "It's just like we're on our way to first period." She sighs. Julie's incredibly nostalgic about high school—even about actual class. Roger and I share a glance in the passenger-side mirror, which he has down while he's fiddling with his hair.

"Too much pomade in those bangs?" I smile.

"Just enough, Miss Greenfield," says Roger, closing up the mirror. "I'm a Dippity Do master these days."

"So, V, how's Chapel Thrill been?" asks Julie as she pulls out of my neighborhood and onto Smith Level Road.

"Snoozeville," I say. "Seriously dead. Richard is like my only friend in town." Richard is the manager at the Palace Theater, where I've worked off-and-on since the summer I was sixteen. He's like thirty-five and completely flamboyant—he loves to hear fashion stories.

"Whoa—hold on!" says Roger. "Violet Greenfield, international runway model, is back to wearing a vest and bow tie?"

"I did *not* take any shifts," I say. And that's sort of true because I haven't worked any regular shifts (although I did sub one day for Benny, a UNC student who works at the Palace, because he needed to drive to Asheville to "score some of that fresh mountain reefer"). But that doesn't count. "I was just visiting people there when I got bored," I clarify.

Roger turns around and raises his eyebrows disbelievingly. "I guess that's what happens when you defer college." He smirks. I punch him on the arm.

"Ouch!" he yells. "Watch the guns!"

I sit back in my seat. I really *had* to defer my admission to Vassar when I got the chance to do some international runway shows this fall. Even though I wanted to quit after my first experiences with the modeling world, I had always dreamed of seeing the world. Let's face it: when you're eighteen and someone hands you a plane ticket to Brazil, and then to Spain, and then to France, you'd have to be a little crazy to turn it down. My dad likes to say that international runways were like my semester-abroad experience. Secretly, though, I think he and Mom are psyched that I'm heading to Vassar in a few weeks to start a traditional college career.

When we get to Elmo's, we grab our usual table in the corner. This is the place the three of us always go to decompress and catch up. I think we love it so much because all of our moms used to take us here when we were really little—it's a kid-friendly diner with crayons and paper to draw on. Roger picks a purple crayon from the cup and starts to sketch his usual—a stick man with an umbrella.

"I see your doodle style hasn't changed," I say, smiling.

"Some things are forever," he says, looking up.

I have to remind myself that Roger is in a relationship now. He's all serious with Chloe—his annoyingly short, blond, and giggly older girlfriend in NYC, who also happens to be an editorial assistant at *Teen Fashionista* magazine. She met Roger when she did a story about me last year, and for some reason she doesn't have a problem dating a college freshman even though she's like twenty-two. Lame. I'm calling them RoChloe behind their backs.

"So what did you do for your birthday?" asks Julie, blowing the paper wrapping of her straw across the table at me and breaking up my bitter thoughts.

"I can't believe we missed your big one-nine," says Roger.

"Strawberry shortcake with the parents and Jake." I sigh. "Nothing monumental."

At the mention of my brother's name, Julie flinches a little bit. "How is Jake?" she asks. Even though he's two years younger than we are, Julie and Jake dated for like six months last year. They broke up at the end of summer when Julie went to college—but not before losing their virginity together. It is completely weird that I know details on my little brother's first time—ew—especially since my own first time hasn't even happened yet.

"He's okay," I say, not really sure what Julie wants to hear. I know he's been dating some girl who's also a junior, but I'm almost positive that information should not be conveyed to Julie right now. She's the one who made the rule that high school relationships end when college begins. I think Jake would have been okay continuing something. Then again, it's not like I've talked to my brother intimately about his emotions—I'm just interpreting various grunts.

"That's cool," says Julie, stirring her iced tea and failing to look nonchalant. "Tell him I say hi."

"I'm sure you'll see him when you come over," I say. "Unless you're planning on avoiding my house for all of break."

She shrugs.

"Jules!" I shout.

"I've heard that maybe he's dating someone else." She looks at me questioningly. "I don't think I want to be around that."

I flash back to the night a couple of months ago when I went to visit Roger in his dorm room in New York, ready to ask him how he really felt about me. When I got to his hallway, I stumbled onto a big party and I saw him and Chloe making out. Pain-ful.

"Okay," I say to Julie. "I'll just come over to your place."

After dinner, on the car ride home, my phone starts ringing. An old Beck song, "Loser," plays scratchily on my outdated cell. I silence it quickly.

"Whoa, who got that diss of a song for their ring?" asks Roger.

"One guess," I say.

"Your agent," says Julie, with total confidence that she's right. And she is.

When the voice mail beep sounds, Roger demands that we listen to the rant on speakerphone. I reluctantly dial up the message.

"Voiceless Violet, always screening my calls," Angela trills. I cringe. Hearing her out loud in the car is pretty scary. "Your semester's starting soon and when you're not chasing gay boys around campus or writing useless drivel about ancient civilizations, we'll need you to be in the city, darling. You've got the Mirabella Prince campaign to promote, and we're counting on you, Veronica and I. Remember, you're still a Tryst Models girl." *Click.*

I sigh audibly.

"Yeesh," says Julie. "Even her voice mail hang-ups sound rude."

"Mirabella Prince is such a ridiculous name," says Roger. "Do you think her real name is something like Myrtle Papadopoulos?"

"No!" I say, laughing. "She's the real deal. In that famous-designer-from-a-rich-family way."

"Sounds so *real*," says Julie, rolling her eyes.

"Are you going to call Angela back?" asks Roger.

"Later," I say, tucking my phone back into my bag.

"I thought you weren't going to model anymore," says Julie. "Didn't you tell her that?"

"Yeah," says Roger. "Isn't this the semester of Violet the Vassar girl, and intellectual beauty who's decidedly *off* the runway?"

"Totally," I say. "She's delusional. I'll call her later and remind her that I'm done."

Roger glances back at me suspiciously, but I just smile. What I can't tell my best friends is that I am terrified of college. And even though I want to, I'm scared to stop modeling. I spent seventeen years of my life not fitting in with anyone except Julie and Roger. Girls were mean to me because I was so freakishly tall and toothpicky, guys ignored me completely, and it wasn't that I was super-smart like Roger or ambitious and involved like Julie. I just sort of blended into the walls.

And I know I'm supposed to be a cultured and worldly nineteen-year-old with sky-high confidence because I've done fashion weeks in New York and three international cities, but the truth is that modeling hasn't raised my self-esteem all that much. It may have even created some new insecurities. Still, if I quit, I'm afraid that I'll revert back to being the girl who was invisible in high school. The girl whose name no one knew. I'm not sure I can risk that.

two

My parents insist on driving me up to Vassar themselves, as if I haven't already lived away from home. "It's a rite of passage," says Mom as we load my new folding bookshelves, two suitcases full of clothes, and various "dorm" items from Bed Bath & Beyond into our station wagon. "It's an excuse for Jake to have a huge party," I say, looking over my shoulder at my little brother, who smiles and puts a finger to his lips to silence me.

Julie left for Brown yesterday, and Roger went up to the city a week early to hang out with Chloe before classes start again. I didn't even listen to one sad song after he left—I am totally focusing on college guys . . . once I meet them.

The drive up I-95 with my parents is actually kind of fun. My dad lets me choose a radio station, and if I can name the titles of five songs in a row before the chorus comes on, I get $5. Jake and I invented this game like five years ago, and usually he's around to compete with me and steal my thunder, so it's nice to play solo. I pocket $10 by the time we get to Virginia, and then Mom requests NPR, so I put on my iPod headphones and lie down in the back-seat, looking out the opposite window at the scraggly pine trees rushing by.

I prop my head on the pillow Mom packed for me, and as I grab a stuffed animal from my bag to cuddle with, I think back to the night when I got coffee with Julie before we said good-bye. I had no idea she was so hung up on my brother, but she really steered clear of our house during all of break. One day when Mom and Dad wanted to ask her how she's doing at Brown, she made them come out to the driveway and stayed in the car while she answered their questions. I finally just brought it up with her directly at Caribou Coffee last week.

"So, are you like in love with Jake still?" I asked her over steam-ing mochas. "Is he the new Funny Monkey?"

She sighed and looked intently at her cup. Funny Monkey is this stuffed chimpanzee of mine that Julie always adored. Since the first night she slept over at my house in kindergarten, we've held Funny Monkey up as the love of both of our lives. In sixth grade, when we both developed a crush on Ben Russell, our secret code name for him was "Funny Monkey." Ben had the most beautiful brown eyes and perfect wavy brown hair. And thinking back now, he had killer bone structure—a strong chin and elegantly masculine cheekbones, especially for an eleven-year-old. I mean, we were heartpoundingly, swooningly in love with him. Then, after sixth grade, he moved. It was the tragedy of our summer that year, and we've held him up as The One (in a half-joking way) ever since.

"It's not that I think he's my new Funny Monkey," Julie said. "It's just that I hate the thought that he's someone else's."

I looked out the window to avoid Julie's gaze.

"Violet, we live in a really small town," she said. "I know he's dating some girl in his class named Katie Fink. Whatever. I just don't want it in my face."

I turned back and looked at her. "Yeah, it sucks," I said.

"Hey, do you still talk to Paulo from São Paulo?" Julie asked, referring to my Brazilian fling from last summer. The fact that I even have a "Brazilian fling" in my past makes me sound much more glam than I ever feel.

"Nah," I said. "I'm so over it."

"So he wasn't the new Funny Monkey either?"

"Not by a long shot," I said. "Maybe I'll meet my Funny Monkey at Vassar."

"Or maybe you've already met him," said Julie. "What if your soul mate is someone you already know. Isn't that weird to think about?"

I tilted my head and looked at her questioningly.

"I guess Roger and Chloe are still going strong," Julie continued, raising her eyebrows.

"Guess so," I said, working to keep my tone even.

"Does that bother you?" she asked.

And even though I knew she knew it bothered me and she wanted me to admit it, I wouldn't. "Nope," I said, standing up to go. "If he wants to go out with a short, honk-laughing girl with no personality, that's his own business."

Julie picked up her cup to follow me out onto the street. "Sounds like you just couldn't care less, V," she said.

I heard the sarcasm in her voice that night, but I decided to ignore it. Sometimes your best friends can read you better than you want them to.

I hug Funny Monkey tighter under my arm and relax with the station wagon's highway rhythm as I drift off to sleep.

As we hit traffic around Philadelphia, my cell phone rings for the third time in the past hour. Luckily, it's not Angela, so I don't have to dodge it.

"Violet," says a husky voice on the other end of the line.

"Veronica!" I'm so happy to hear from my old roommate. She completely saved my ass this fall when I wanted to bail from the Mirabella Prince campaign. She convinced Mirabella that she and I should work the shoot together as a team. That meant I got to go home early—which I really needed.

"Where are you?" she asks.

"Um, in the car with my parents," I say. Mom turns around and exaggeratedly mouths *SAY HELLO*, so I know she's listening.

"They say hi," I tell Veronica.

"Hi back," she says. "So, did you enjoy being home in the sticks?"

"It beats the pressures of the big city," I reply.

"That pressure's only going to get more intense when the Mirabella campaign breaks next month," says Veronica, sounding giddy. For both of us, this is like the biggest modeling job we've ever done. Being the face of a prestigious designer's campaign can mean total fame and fortune on the Kate Moss level. But just thinking about it makes my stomach cramp up.

"Yeah, I guess," I say.

"And you'll be down in the city sometimes, right?" she asks. "I mean, don't tell me I'm going to be without the other half of the Double V for much longer!"

"Well, Vassar's not exactly in midtown Manhattan," I say. Pough-keepsie is two hours north of New York City. It's not really a college town like Chapel Hill—I've heard that students don't hang out in Poughkeepsie much, so maybe it'll be nice to take the train down to the city every so often.

"Believe me," she says. "You'll be ready to bust out of that campus every weekend."

"And I guess you'll be at Grand Central to greet me and lead me to the hottest parties in town?" I ask.

"You got it!" says Veronica.

Dad eyes me in the rearview mirror, but I just stick my tongue out at him to let him know that I'm joking. Sort of. Last year Veronica and I got a reputation around town as "the Double V"—all these New York newspapers wrote about our clubbing escapades. When Veronica had to go into rehab, though, those same papers that had been celebrating her tore her apart. I guess that's the nature of the press, but it was a big wake-up call for me. The party circuit is not one that I want to get back into this year.

"So listen, have you seen today's *New York Post*?" Veronica asks.

"I hate that question," I say.

"Don't be upset—but let me just read you something," says Veronica. Then she puts on her teacher voice:

Violet Greenfield, who made both her New York and inter-national debut last year, is starting as a freshman at Vassar this week. With one of fashion's most promising talents busy studying in Poughkeepsie, will Tryst Models be able to make a splash at February's Fashion Week? Stay tuned.

"Great," I say. "That must be why I had to dodge two more calls from Angela today."

"Don't worry, Violet," says Veronica. But then she adds, "Just promise me you'll get to the city for some Mirabella Prince promotion."

"I will." I sigh. I know I'll have to do at least a few appearances with Veronica for this campaign.

Veronica must hear my exasperation, because she totally changes gears.

"So, anyway, how was it being at home?" she asks. "Did you confess your love to the boy wonder?"

Veronica has this theory that I've been in love with Roger for years and I'm just in denial.

"Nah," I say, trying to sound nonchalant. "I'm looking forward to meeting some, um, other people."

I eye Mom and Dad, but they're just staring straight ahead and listening to NPR.

"You mean straight guys?" laughs Veronica. "The ratio's against you." Vassar has more girls than guys, and lots of guys who like guys, too, but I'm not letting the odds get me down.

"I'll use my supermodel charm," I joke. "These boys will be putty in my hands."

"I have no doubts, Greenfield," says Veronica.

After we hang up, Mom turns around and says, "I always liked that Veronica Trask. Is she doing okay?"

I don't tell my parents much, but I might have let it slip that I helped Veronica through some drug issues last year.

"She's doing great now," I say, and I mean it. My former nemesis has truly become one of my best friends.

When we get to Vassar, it's pretty late. Dad takes care of getting my key from a security guy, and my parents spend an hour helping me bring my stuff into my dorm room. Then they each give me big hugs, and I'm surprised to find myself fighting back tears.

Saying good-bye to Mom and Dad is oddly sad. I left them last year to move to NYC and live in a model apartment, which should have ostensibly been much scarier than moving into a dorm room in college where I'm surrounded by people my own age who all want to make friends. But maybe I'm tearing up because college feels bizarrely like camp, which I never enjoyed. It's a bunch of people your own age, yes, but they're people who are judging you, figuring out if you're cool enough, immediately establishing your social position. It might be even more vicious than fashion.

As I watch my parents walk down the extra-wide hallway of my dorm, I swallow the lump in my throat. I wave one last time and head back into my room. It's actually a suite in a dorm called Main, which is—as its name suggests—the big, prominent building on campus. It's the original postcard portrait of Vassar, and it has dorm rooms, but also the college center downstairs and lots of administrative offices, as well as the Rose Parlor, where they serve tea every weekday at four p.m. Mom *loved* that when she heard about it, but I'm not sure it's something I'll be attending.

The suite is big—there's a living room with a futon couch and a table, and there are three bedrooms off the common area. No one else seems to be here, but the common space is sparsely decorated with a bizarre Vassar Film League calendar, one of those old World War II posters of Rosie the Riveter (thank you, AP American History class), and a large, mostly dead, green-brown plant in the corner. I'm tempted to peek into the other rooms, but the doors are closed and I'm afraid I'll get caught snooping, even though I'm here a day early. Tomorrow everyone will be back from winter break for real. I just wanted a night to feel the campus out for myself.

I walk into my small bedroom and wonder who had it last semester. There are still pushpins in the walls and a couple of wire hangers in the beat-up armoire. Maybe this person couldn't handle the work and dropped out. Maybe something really tragic happened in her family and she had to go home. Maybe my suitemates are total bitches and the roommate couldn't deal.

Julie's life coach would so not approve of this negative thinking.

I decide to call my aunt Rita in Brooklyn. She's a quirky one—she runs a pottery shop out of her backyard—but she always knows what to say.

"Hi, Rita," I say when she picks up the phone.

"Violet!" she says, sounding genuinely happy to hear from me. "How's my girl?"

"Good," I say, feeling a sniffle start to come. "I just got to Vassar and Mom and Dad left, so I'm kind of—"

She interrupts me before my voice cracks. "Scared and apprehensive?" she asks.

"Yes," I say, smiling despite my urge to cry.

"It's normal," she says, going into her no-nonsense, that's-the-way-it-is voice. She tells me about how on her first night alone after she moved out of her parents' house, she curled up in a ball among the boxes and cried herself to sleep.

"Pathetic, right?" she says, laughing at herself. "But that apartment turned out to be the best and bravest move I ever made. College is F-U-N, kid."

When we hang up, I feel much better. I also want to make sure I don't spend *my* night curled up crying among unpacked boxes—it does sound dismal.

I lift my suitcase onto the ultra-narrow bed. There's a window in my room, but it leads into the hallway. It's that mottled glass that people sometimes have in their bathroom windows so people can't see through them but light can still come in. I'd prefer the room with the outdoor view, but I'm coming into this living situation late, so I don't have much say. I take out two pairs of shoes and start to arrange them in the closet when I hear the door to the suite fling open.

"I'm back, bitches!" yells a shrill voice outside my room. "Who wants a shot?!" A tall, thin blond guy wearing a super-tight shirt that has a picture of a match and the word *Flamer* on it appears in my doorway.

"Oh," he says, curling his lip. "Who are you?"

"I'm, um, Violet," I stammer, feeling like I've already disappointed the first person I'm meeting at college just by not being whoever he was expecting.

"Hi," he says, "I'm Kurt. I was looking for Fan and Jess, but I guess they're not back yet. So you're replacing Amy, huh? Good thing—just between us, she was a major psycho. Ooh, you're like really tall. Do you play basketball?"

"Nope." I laugh. "So was Amy really crazy?" I want to detract attention from my freakish height, and I'm glad to be included in any sort of gossip.

"Yeah," Kurt says, coming into my room and sitting down on my bare mattress. "And not someone who brought the good kind of drama. Fan and I used to say that the girl was majoring in cuckoo. In fact, I'd Febreze everything in here if I were you. Including the hangers."

"Fan?" I ask.

"Yeah, as in *the blades that cool you down in the summer*," he says. "She's one of your suitemates, a Filipina punk who's totally green."

Before I can ask what that means, exactly, Kurt leans over and peeks into my suitcase, reaching in to pull out my Christian Louboutin dust bag. "Oooh," he says with wonder. "May I?"

"Um, those are kind of—" I start, but before I can finish, Kurt has whipped out my glitter-red five-inch designer heels. He gasps audibly.

"Oh *my*," he says, standing up and slipping off his own shoes. "Are you some sort of *Wizard of Oz* It girl?"

"No," I say, feeling my face turn red. Why did I pack those heels anyway? Angela wanted me to buy them for an event last year, but what was I thinking bringing them to college with me? I'm sure they will never be appropriate attire here. And now Kurt thinks I'm weird.

Of course, he's the one who took off his shoes and is trying on my size 11 Louboutins, so maybe I'm not the most eccentric one in the room. He stumbles a bit and grabs onto my shoulder for balance.

"Oh my God! I know who you are!" he screams, narrowing his eyes at me as he kicks off the heels. Then he runs out of the room in a shot.

I'm flabbergasted, but before I have a chance to even wonder where Kurt went, he's back. And he's holding an issue of *Nylon* from last summer. "Violet Greenfield, I presume. Page eighty-two. I didn't recognize you at first with that dishwater hair and those silly flip-flops—and boy, do you need that eye makeup to get those gray orbs to pop, but you clean up good, girl! This is you."

I nod, glancing briefly at the spread in *Nylon* that Kurt is pointing at—it's the one that I shot last spring when I had a crazy-dark purple smoky eye and I had to wear a sheer top—you can totally see my nipple. Of course *that's* the issue that he has to have with him. It couldn't be the innocent *Teen Girl* shoot where I'm showcasing jumpsuits and umbrellas?

"I love it!" squeals Kurt, throwing down the magazine and diving back into my suitcase. "Let me help you unpack, Miss Supermodel. I have a feeling we are going to be BFFAA."

"BFFAA?" I ask, raising an eyebrow.

"Best friends forever and always, duh!"

I smile. I think Rita might be right about college.

three

I wake up the next morning to an eerie si-
lence on the hall. My clock says nine-sixteen a.m. Early! What is
wrong with my sleep schedule? I stayed up past two a.m. with Kurt,
who I've decided is fantastic. I'm aware that it's partly the modeling
thing that interests him, but I also think we have similar senses of
humor. Besides, he can bring me out of my shell. He's so incredibly
extroverted that hanging out with him might mean that I don't have
a shell at all—or at least that I can hide my shyness here and be a
better, more confident version of myself. After all, no one knows
me yet.

I decide to post a new blog on myspace.com/violetgreenfield. I
built a fan base last year, and now I sort of feel responsible to keep
my "friends" up on what's going on—better people hear it from me
than wonder about the *New York Post*'s speculations.

I open up my laptop, log on, and see that there are a few pages of
new friend requests. I was pretty good about approving everyone

while I was home, but they're piling up again. I make a mental note to get to those soon. Then I start to blog:

> So I'm in college now! And by "in college," I mean I'm physically sitting in my dorm room at Vassar. I'm really, really glad I'm here, but I know maybe some of you are wondering if I'm going to keep modeling this year. Well, I have a big campaign coming out soon for Mirabella Prince, so I hope you like it! Thanks for all the friend requests—I promise to catch up on everything soon!

There, that should make Veronica and Angela happy—I plugged the campaign even though I have mixed feelings about its "Healthy Body" message. I sort of feel like a hypocrite about the whole thing—you know, the tall-and-skinny-by-nature girl who's telling other people to love their bodies?

When I started blogging, I used to write about some private stuff. I even put up things about Roger, though I never mentioned his name. I feel a tiny bit guilty that this post is boring and generic, but I have a lot more people friending me and reading the blogs now, so it's also super-public.

I close my laptop and stand up to look around the room. Kurt helped me get all of my clothes unpacked and even taped some photos to my mirror—high school shots with Julie and Roger, and a couple of Polaroids of me and Veronica . . . Still, the aging glass doesn't feel quite decorated enough.

I pull my suitcase out from under my bed and reach into the small interior pocket, where I stashed a small, wrinkled piece of yellow paper—a poem from Spain. It's just two lines of verse written in Spanish: *No mas que amigos; no menos que amor verdadero*—"No more than friends; no less than true love." Roger bought it from a street vendor when we were traveling in Barcelona. He had it in his mirror at NYU before I took it, and now I want it on mine. I tuck it casually into the bottom right corner of the frame to remind me of . . . I don't know what. A time when I was with my best friend in a foreign country and there was something so electric in the air that we actually *kissed*. A time when I didn't know how I felt about him, so I ran away and left him stranded. A time when—

"Ooomph!" My about-to-turn-irrecoverably-sappy thoughts are interrupted by the sound of heavy lifting.

I grab my glasses and peek out the bedroom door to find a tiny, freckle-faced girl with wispy brown hair and a birdlike nose trying to move a gigantic suitcase into the far bedroom.

"Can I help with that?" I ask, smiling and hoping that my chipper-in-the-morning attitude will win me a friend in the suite. Of course, I'm faking it. I am so not chipper in the morning.

"Got it," says Bird Girl, positioning herself against the hefty luggage and propelling it into her room with the force of her entire petite body. "There!" She stands up straight and wipes her hands on her jeans. "I'm Jess."

"Violet," I say.

The door to the suite bursts open before Jess and I can exchange any more information. "JJ!" shrieks Kurt as he rushes over and swings Jess around. "Oh my God—did you meet your new supermodel roommate? Isn't she a dream? Yummy. Let's go be seen together on campus—you guys wanna grab breakfast at ACDC?"

ACDC is the cafeteria at Vassar. I found that out through the marathon of Vassar trivia that Kurt went over with me last night, and he also told me that ACDC has a cameo in the movie *The Muppets Take Manhattan*. Who knew?

"Let me just change," I say, feeling glad that I actually have people to eat with on day one. Huge victory. Maybe it won't be so bad being the new girl.

When I head into the bathroom to brush my teeth, there's a guy standing at the sink with a towel wrapped around his waist. Let me be more specific: there's an extremely attractive, *ripped* guy with shaggy blond hair and huge blue eyes standing at the sink half naked. I look down at the off-white tile floor and head to the far sink, feeling my face flush.

Then I hear a girl's voice. "Josh! You used up all the hot water!" A cute brunette with perfectly shaped eyebrows emerges from the shower in a towel. She walks right up to shaggy hot guy and pulls him to her, kissing him on the mouth. Whoa. I knew the bathrooms here were co-ed, but I didn't know they were *this* co-ed. I skip flossing and exit the bathroom as soon as I finish brushing.

"What happened?" says Kurt when I get back down the hall. "You look traumatized."

"I guess the co-showering thing is new to me," I say, not wanting to sound like a prude but still kinda scandalized.

"Ew!" shouts Kurt. Then he turns his head down the hall toward the bathroom. "Josh and Brianna—get a room, for God's sakes! You're scaring the transfers!" Then he claps his hand over his mouth like he can't believe he just said that. "I'm so bad," he whispers.

Josh sticks his head out of the bathroom. "Fuck off, Kurt!"

I'm mortified, but Kurt's giggle is infectious. "Come on, let's go eat!" he shouts.

Jess, Kurt, and I walk through a wooded area on a path to ACDC. The campus is movie-set beautiful—old brick buildings with ivy growing up the sides, perfectly pristine snow-covered lawns, a giant Gothic library with stained glass all over the place. I think it was the aesthetic that I fell for primarily. Is that bad? I'm sure the classes will be good too. It's *freezing* here, but so pretty that I almost don't care.

"So Kurt mentioned you're a model?" asks Jess, turning to look up at me.

"Yeah," I say slowly, hoping that's not weird. It's kind of weird. I know that.

"*Hello*, JJ! Not just a model, but like a hugely successful Tryst Model!" Kurt beams over at me and skips ahead of us, turning around and walking backward through the snow like a tour guide. "Violet, you should know that most people here have their heads so far up their liberally educated asses that they won't recognize you and give you the attention you deserve. Either that, or they'll pretend not to know who you are because they're jealous and they don't like to acknowledge fame. JJ is just one of the former—she really has no clue."

"Shut up!" shouts Jess, laughing. "Just because I don't reserve the TV for *American's Next Top Tyra* doesn't mean I'm totally ignorant." She rolls her eyes in my direction. "This shit coming from the guy who throws out the whole Sunday *New York Times* after he reads the Style section."

"I gotta keep up with Bill Cunningham and the wedding announcements, bitch!" shouts Kurt. "Now stop being so aggro. You're scaring Violet. Don't worry, V, everyone is gonna love you!"

I smile and shrug. "I'll just be glad if no one makes fun of my height," I say.

"Oh my God, Violet," says Kurt, looking at me with widened eyes. "You are so stuck in high school. Isn't she, Jess? That was just like a high school insecurity laid at our feet!"

"Kurt, high school was only six months ago for all of us," says Jess.

"I know, but we've come so far!" sings Kurt, leaping ahead on the path and up the stairs to the dining hall.

I look over at Jess. *Did I really just sound like a high school kid?* I'm so lame for exposing my insecurities right away. It's like I have insecurity Tourette's or something—they just spill out of me for the world to see. Ugh.

"Don't worry," says Jess. "Kurt just likes to be dramatic. But he's right about one thing, Violet: high school's over."

four

My first week of college has been pretty great. Intro to Sociology is my favorite class so far. The focus is the media's effect on today's youth. So it's like everyone in the class is constantly discussing pop culture's effect on themselves. People here raise their hands all the time and they practically battle each other to speak. Jess was right—it's so not high school.

It's also not the modeling world. Jess and our other suitemate, Fan, are scarily perfect to live with. Fan's this punk-rocker girl from Baltimore who has a shaved head with just a little tuft of bleached blond hair in the middle—she's from the Philippines, but she's lived in the United States since she was five, and she's really into all things environmental—like she only uses totally green beauty products. When I first saw her, I was nervous that she might be too cool for me, but after hanging out for meals and just kind of existing in the same space, I realize that she's smart and nice and not so sweet that she's boring, but not so snarky that you feel like you have to watch your back, either. I guess living with Veronica and Sam, our third model roommate, in NYC last year was a trial-by-fire situation. Between Sam traveling all the time for modeling jobs in Miami and Veronica's cocaine habit and eating issues, I think I've paid my roommate dues. I still love Sam and Veronica, but I have to admit that it's nice to be around normal people who aren't competing with me or judging me all the time.

It's Thursday afternoon, and when I get back from English class, Fan and Jess are heading out to put up posters around campus that promote environmental awareness.

"Basically, my first mission is to try to stop these water-chugging bitches from tossing ten bottles a day," Fan explains.

I look guiltily at the Poland Spring collection building up in the common room.

"Well, you at least refill yours a few times," Fan says. "Baby steps."

I drop off my books and decide to join them. The three of us step outside into the crisp winter air and walk toward the chapel, where Fan wants us to tape flyers on the doors and also slip some into the pews. "Anyone who has enough guilt to go to church during college will definitely feel guilty not protecting the earth," she says. "At least they should."

"Violet, what religion are you?" asks Jess, looking up at me as we walk along the sidewalk. I've noticed that she has this habit of asking big questions in a nonchalant way, but I don't really mind.

"I went to a Methodist church when I was younger, but I haven't been to services besides Easter and Christmas Eve for a while," I admit. "My mom and dad let me and my brother choose whether to go after we turned thirteen. And we kind of chose not going."

"That's cool," says Jess, looking ahead thoughtfully.

"What about you?" I ask her.

"I'm Jewish," she says. "And Fan's agnostic."

"That makes our suite religiously diverse," says Fan, smiling. "One confused Filipina, a lapsed Methodist, and a total heeb!"

I look over at Jess, and she's laughing as she reaches out her arm to hit Fan with her stack of flyers.

After an hour of covering half the campus with environmentally responsible messages, I have to ask Fan if spreading all this paper around is really in keeping with her green policies.

"It's recycled paper," she says, shrugging. "Now let's go get snacks for tonight."

I grin. My suitemates and I have fallen into a Thursday-night routine of playing this drinking game called Mexicali that involves two dice, a little bluffing, and a *lot* of beer and junk food. It's the total opposite of a calorie-counting model drink night, where everyone's ordering rum and Diet Coke, but maybe that's why I love it.

As we walk to the deli, Jess says, "Fan, show Violet your fake ID."

"No way," says Fan. "We won't even need it."

"Not the point!" says Jess, reaching into Fan's back pocket and swiftly pulling out her wallet, which is a cool metallic patchwork design.

"It's made from recycled candy wrappers," says Fan, noticing my admiring look.

Jess holds up a driver's license and waves it in front of my face. I steady her hand so I can get a good look at it.

"Jasper Wong, 52 Simsbury Road, West Granby, Connecticut . . ." I read aloud. "This is a middle-aged man!"

Jess cackles with delight while Fan grabs the license.

"He's only twenty-seven," says Fan, stuffing Jasper's ID back into her wallet.

"He's balding!" Jess laughs.

"Hey, that thing has worked for me twice," says Fan, smiling.

"So does that mean if someone's not really looking, you could pass for an old guy from Connecticut?" I ask.

"Watch it, Greenfield," says Fan. She's laughing while she says it, though.

"Please say you'll let me scan that into my blog," I say.

"Only if you'll get the treats for tonight," says Fan, as we walk into the deli.

I feel a happy buzz—it's nice to hang out with new friends and not be talking about our weight or which photo shoots we have coming up. This feels normal. It feels like real life.

On Sunday, I sleep until noon and only venture downstairs to get a bagel from the Retreat, a campus food spot that's actually *in* my dorm. I have a lot of reading already, and I'm lying on my bed trying to focus on the required book from my English 101 class when I hear Kurt coming down the hall. He's hard to miss, wherever he is. Kurt is always shouting or whooping or laughing at incredibly high volumes. It annoys some people on campus, I've noticed, but most people—including me—think he's a blast. He's like my best friend here.

"Violet Greenfield—the new face of Mirabella!" He bursts into the suite, which is never locked, with an issue of *Vogue* in his hand. "I just got my subscription copy!" he yells, breathing heavily. He must have run all the way upstairs from his mailbox in the Main College Center. "It's probably been on newsstands for three days already! Violet! Why didn't you *tell* me?!"

And it's strange, because I'm not sure why I didn't mention this giant campaign to my new friends. Or why I haven't told them about walking runways in São Paulo, Madrid, Paris, New York . . . or why

I haven't mentioned that my agent's been calling me daily to ask when I can work. Angela has started to address me as "Violet the Villain-ess," which I think means she's pretty mad that I'm ignoring her at the moment. Every time Kurt tries to grill me about modeling, I find some way to turn the subject back to him. (He's sort of self-involved, so this trick works well.) And the truth is that I am blocking out that part of my life. I don't want to be Violet on the Runway right now—I want my own, normal, Violet Greenfield existence. I want to study sociology and read great works of literature and even learn a little econ to fulfill my quantitative requirement. I want to spend long hours in the library and go to campus parties and talk to my profes-sors during their office hours. I want to be a real college kid.

But I have to admit that as Kurt dangles the *Vogue* in front of my face, I can't help but be curious. "Does it look good?" I ask.

"Are you insane?! It looks *ah-mazing*!" Kurt says, sitting beside me on the bed and opening up the issue.

I stare down at the page. Okay, the campaign does look stunning. My hair is in this Veronica Lake–style blowout, so it covers one eye. I flash back to the shoot—how desperately bored I felt, how I wanted nothing more than to leave Paris that day, how empty my heart was. But somehow—digital imaging, maybe?—the photo-graph completely works. I'm sitting on a Lucite chair with my legs closed at the knee but then splayed at an awkward angle from the shin down. My toes are turned in, which gives the image a childlike feeling, and my posture from the waist up is confident and strong. But what really makes the look come together is my expression. How did bored, empty, and desperate turn into the quiet intensity in this photo? I look brave, powerful, soft, and vulnerable all at the same time. In spite of myself, I start to smile.

Kurt breathes a huge sigh. "Oh, thank God," he says. "You like

it. I thought you were going to go into some woeful model mono-
logue about how the angle made your ankles look fat."

"It's pretty," I say. "I mean, with makeup and hair and lighting
and a great photographer, they can make anyone look kind of *ah-
mazing*."

"Okay, modest mouse," says Kurt, rolling his eyes. "Please. You're
gorgeous. I see guys checking you out all day long on campus. Even
the guys who should be checking *me* out look at you first. Fashion
whores!" He giggles and grabs the magazine from me, standing up.

Then he looks back at the page and starts reading: "'I am a real
girl. I love my body because it is strong. I love my body because it is
healthy. I love my body because it is beautiful.' Did you really say
that?"

"Ick, no!" I wince, lying back on my bed and covering my face
with a pillow so my voice is muffled. "Mirabella wanted her campaign to have this mission statement about healthy body image. She
and my agent pretty much made me sign on for that."

"Oh, I'm anti–healthy body image too," says Kurt, putting his
hand on his hip.

"No, no!" I say, throwing off the pillow. "It's just that I didn't
want to do this big fashion campaign as a size 0 girl who starved herself to fit into the sample sizes at the shoot while there was this con-
tradictory Love Your Body message tied to it!"

I grab the magazine back from him and look at the ad again. The
quote is pretty small, but it definitely has my name attached to it, and
I see minuscule text at the bottom that directs people to Mirabella's
website, where there's apparently information on some campaign for
positive body image.

"What a joke!" I shout, pointing the small print out to Kurt.
"She made me lose weight before I could officially book her runway

show last year!" I can feel my heart start to race as I stare up at him. Kurt is completely rapt.

"Really?" he asks fascinated. "What else happened? I read that Veronica Trask got this campaign."

"She did," I say, closing the magazine and willing myself to calm down. "I mean, I did first. And then we both did. Sort of."

I explain to Kurt how I had the campaign but then I just wanted to bolt. Veronica came to my rescue, concocting a plan where she would also be a part of the campaign—we'd share it. I smile at remembering how sneaky Veronica even got Mirabella to think it was her own idea to let us share the campaign.

"Oooh, Veronica Trask sounds like an evil genius!" says Kurt, rubbing his hands together in delight.

"She pretty much is," I say.

"So when can I meet her?" he asks.

"Sometime maybe," I say, being vague and suddenly so not wanting to further this conversation. I just don't want to think about last fall and all the emotions I went through. I was trying to deal with my own body issues—at eighteen, even the toothpick girl's metabolism started to slow a little—and trying to figure out if the modeling world was what I really wanted. I decided it wasn't. Which is why I haven't returned Angela's calls this week. Or Veronica's, for that matter.

"So Gregory Danner missed English last week," I say to Kurt, knowing that the mention of his crush's name will divert his attention instantly.

"Oooh, where was he?" coos Kurt, completely forgetting about Veronica and the Mirabella campaign and my modeling career. "I wonder if he's sick! Should I buy some chicken soup and walk it over to Lathrop?"

Kurt's been stalking Gregory since first semester. It's this epic drama, according to Jess and Fan. Gregory lives in Lathrop House, a dorm that's a quick walk down the quad from Main.

"I think you should," I say, smiling.

"Come with?" asks Kurt. "It'll be so less obvious if you're there. Just promise you'll leave if he takes off my pants."

I laugh and stand up, linking arms with him. "Sure," I say. "I could use a break from *Tristram Shandy* anyway. This guy just goes on and on about his own nose."

Kurt tosses *Vogue* on the bed and we walk out the door. I glance back at the magazine worriedly, but then I realize that no one has really even recognized me as being a model. I've gotten a few tall comments, but it's not like people here are obsessed with who's walking which runway and which It girl is the toast of the season. We're in yoga pants and hoodies, walking around a wintry campus and trying to finish lengthy, involved, analytical papers about long-dead scholars and philosophers. No one pays attention to the frivolous fashion world, I assure myself.

And just like that, I'm back to being a college girl. *Phew.*

The next day in Sociology, I realize that I underestimated pop culture's reach. Turns out that the Vassar campus is extremely plugged in—and lots of students get *Vogue*. In fact, I see three people carrying the March issue under their arms as I walk into class. My palms start to sweat.

The *Vogue* carriers sit together in the front corner of the room. When Professor Kirby walks in five minutes late, one of them immediately starts talking.

"Professor Kirby, I have something I want to bring up in class today," she says. I stare at her brown, thick-heeled Mary Janes as she stands up with her magazine. She's wearing black wool tights and a plaid mini-dress. *Does this über-intellectual type read* Vogue? Maybe just for the cultural criticism.

And then she opens the issue to an earmarked page.

"I came across this ad yesterday," she starts, now addressing the entire classroom. My pulse quickens. "It's for the spring Mirabella Prince campaign. While it doesn't look very different from all the other fashion ads we're seeing in magazines today, this one is particularly insidious."

I've noticed that people here love using words like *insidious*. And *duplicitous*. And my personal favorite, *Machiavellian*. Yeah, I know what those words mean, but I'm not gonna slip them into discussion. A paper, maybe, but out loud? I know Roger would wince with me.

But Miss Mary Janes keeps talking and dropping SAT words as she goes on about how the ad features "a very thin model who's promoting a particularly harmful and hypocritical healthy body message," and I realize that there's no one here to wince with me. I am alone—and under attack.

I stare at Miss Mary Jane's straight black bangs. I don't want to look in her eyes, but I also don't want to look away. It's not clear whether she's aware of the fact that I'm in the ad. She hasn't said anything directly to me yet, and the photo is so glam that it's certainly a contrast to the puffy-coat-and-fleece uniform that I've been wearing around campus. Maybe no one knows. Maybe no one has to know.

When the Mary Janes girl takes a breath, a guy named Oliver chimes in. He sits in the back and hasn't said much so far this semester. But for some reason, he's on top of this one. "I agree that the juxtaposition of a stick-thin model and a healthy body campaign may seem strange on a basic level," he starts. "But who are we to say that this model doesn't have a healthy body? Was she born to be a size zero? Some people are. How can we presume that she has an eating disorder or other unhealthy habits just because she's skinny?"

I'm starting to like this Oliver guy.

"That's not the point!" shouts one of the other *Vogue* toters, holding up her own copy for emphasis. "It doesn't matter whether this girl is naturally thin or not. What matters is that women are going to see this image—one that they're seeing as the unequivocal standard of beauty right now—and feel the need to starve themselves to look like her. It's like this Mirabella ad is trying to say that not only is being skin-and-bones a requirement for high fashion, but it's also now being equated with being healthy and loving your body, which is absurd!"

I sit through another diatribe from Rachel in the seat next to mine, and another from Jordan over by the window. It seems like all twenty-five people in this class have something to say about the ad. Most of them agree that it's a negative message to be conveying to women, but everyone wants to say it in their own way with their own SAT words. It's painful.

I keep my head up and my eyes on the whiteboard in front of me. Professor Kirby is sitting on the side of his desk, eyes shining, as the students lead the discussion. When I finally let myself glance at the clock, I sigh with relief as I realize there are only three minutes left in class.

And then, Oliver in the back row pipes up again. "I'd like to know what Violet thinks."

Let me rescind that thought about liking Oliver. Twenty-five pairs of eyes are on me. My face turns bright red—I can feel the heat—and I stutter, "It's just a fashion ad."

The room is silent, waiting for me to say more. I see the *Vogue* subscribers whispering, and I realize I've been kidding myself. Everyone knows that it's me in the ad. I look to Professor Kirby for help, but he's looking back, waiting for an explanation.

I want to curl up and die.

Finally, after thirty seconds that feel like ten years, Professor Kirby breaks the silence. "Okay." He claps his hands together. "We're out of time for today, folks. Great discussion—I love to see you bringing topics to class, Miss Harrison." He nods at the Mary Janes girl. "This particular topic touches on a lot of ideas we're covering this semester. Everyone pick up a copy of *Vogue* and take a close look at the ad. We'll be addressing the issue again soon." He smiles at me as I pick up my notebook and head for the door. He doesn't seem to know that this hour was excruciating, humiliating, and terrorizing for me. He seems to think it must have been fun, exciting, and interesting to be at the center of a theoretically "academic" discussion. He's an emotional moron.

When I get back to my suite, I don't even check to see if Fan and Jess are in their rooms. I flop down onto my bed and bury my head in my pillow. This semester just got a lot more complicated.

five

In the middle of my pity party, the phone rings. Caller ID says "V2"—Veronica. I've been diss-buttoning her all week because I want to get settled into college life before I talk to her, but right now I feel like I could use her advice.

"Hey," I say, picking up the phone with a sniffle.

"What's wrong?" she asks. "A cold from the Poughkeepsie winter already?"

"Just a rough day," I say.

"Spill," she commands.

I fight back the tears as I tell Veronica all about what happened in Sociology.

"Academic assholes," she says curtly. "They're jealous."

"No," I say. "I don't think that's it."

"Of course it is!" she asserts. "They have no knowledge of fashion, no reference point for great photography, and I'm willing to bet not one of them has a good sense of style."

I chuckle remembering Miss Mary Janes's outfit. But then I feel guilty for judging her, so I shut up.

"V, is school really where you want to be?" presses Veronica. "I know you haven't been answering Angela's calls—or mine, for that matter. She's been riding my ass about when you're available for go-sees, and with this campaign just breaking you're going to be getting a *lot* of requests."

I look up at a photo of me, Veronica, and Sam that we took last year in Paris. We're in the garden of the Rodin Museum, in front of a huge rose bush and a famous statue (don't ask me which one—I'm bad with art). Point is: it's gorgeous and sunny and we look fabulous. Modeling was really thrilling at times, and I got the opportunity to travel and see amazing places and meet people in different parts of the world. But then I think about how I mostly stayed in my hotel room in Paris, and how I was eating so poorly that I almost fainted on the Métro, and how Veronica was a big part of that behavior.

"I'm done with modeling," I say.

"I've heard that before," says Veronica.

It's true—I tried to quit last summer before Angela called me and told me that Dona Pink, an up-and-coming designer, had asked me to walk his show in Brazil.

"I want to be a student," I say. "I'm just a regular girl on campus now. It's nice."

"A regular girl?" says Veronica, snorting. "Yeah, right, V. Hide under a puffy coat all you want—it's obvious that people have noticed you. You're Violet Greenfield, the girl who rocked Paris Fashion Week. Do you really want to go back to being that insecure girl from North Carolina?"

"No," I say, getting annoyed. "But I don't want to go back to being that peer-pressured wimp of a girl who couldn't stand up for her beliefs in Paris last fall. I never should have done the Mirabella campaign—you know that."

"Well, you did it," says Veronica. "And I'm sure you're not about to give back your fee, since it's probably paying the Vassar bill. So deal. Besides, who cares? It's just a freaking *fashion shoot!*"

"That was my defense in class," I say, starting to laugh.

"Good one!" says Veronica sarcastically. "I'm sure all the over-achieving overreactors accepted that explanation."

"Not quite," I say.

"Well, whatever," says Veronica. "Chin up, V. And come down to the city soon. I swear I won't tell Angela you're around if you'd rather lay low."

"Maybe," I say, unconvinced.

"You could see Roger," says Veronica, teasing me. My eyes dart to the piece of yellow paper taped to my mirror.

"We'll see," I say, considering it. I mean, I don't have Friday classes so I could go down for a three-day weekend if I wanted. Maybe it would be a good break.

When I hang up, I feel a teensy bit better about things. Veronica is so black-and-white about the modeling world. She goes for what she wants and makes no apologies. Sometimes I wish I were ruthless like that.

I head to the bathroom and press a washcloth to my face, trying to make my puffy eyes go down before anyone sees me. It's almost time for dinner.

That night at the dining hall, Kurt eyes me suspiciously as Jess and Fan join us at a table.

"Did you nap recently?" he asks.

"Yes," I say.

"So that's why your face has little crushed pillow marks on it?" He dips his fork into a container of ranch before stabbing a pile of iceberg lettuce. That's his portion control method for salad dressing (and I thought I was the one with the body issues).

"Yes," I say. "I just woke up like right before you came to get us for dinner."

"Dude, Violet," says Fan, jerking up her head so that the swatch of bleached hair flies out of her face. "We heard you crying earlier."

Jess nods.

I sigh.

"Tell Dear Abby, princess," says Kurt. "What's the deal?"

I start to explain about the Mirabella ad, but when I talk about it, it all sounds so weird and braggy. I mean, what exactly am I supposed to say? "So when I was in Paris last year for the shows, I got hired for this huge campaign—which by the way is paying for my tuition, so I have no loans. Aren't you jealous?" I avoid the money stuff, and I leave out anything that sounds remotely glamorous— it just seems obnoxious to bring up—but I do confess to major hypocrisy last year.

My lasagna remains untouched as I talk nonstop. I stare at the back of the dining hall, toward the windows, so I don't have to look at my new friends' widening eyes. I know I'm telling a story they didn't expect to hear. "So even though I'd spoken to the press about how I thought girls should have a healthy body image and shouldn't be subjected to the pressures that the modeling world can put out there, I starved myself so that I could get into Mirabella's good graces. And then I let her use my face as a promotional tool so that she could pretend to be on the healthy body train. And now I'm getting called on it."

I tell them about Sociology, and how the ad was actually used as a visual prop in class. And how I clammed up and couldn't even think of a way to defend myself.

"Yowza!" says Kurt when I finish. Jess lets out a breath and looks down at her grilled cheese. But Fan pipes up right away. "And now you're done with modeling, right?" she says, leaning over to sip her fifth soda of the day. She keeps our mini-fridge stocked with Dr Pepper. It's crazy.

I look back at her, but I don't say anything for a few seconds. *Am I done? Like* done *done? As in, never-walk-a-runway-or-pose-for-a-camera-again done?* "Yes, I'm done," I say. It comes out sounding like a lie, and I think it might be.

"Well, then you have no problem," says Fan. "You can tell your classmates that you recognized the hypocrisy of the ad and that you quit modeling just after it was shot. They should respect that."

Kurt clicks his tongue.

"You disagree, Sir Sound Effect?" asks Fan.

"I don't think Violet owes anyone that," he says, looking over at me. "I mean, unless you want to explain things. I think you should tell Professor Kirby that you appreciate the topic of discussion but that you're uncomfortable with the focus on you personally. I mean, *hello*, your classmates completely blindsided you today. It was super-wrong."

"He's right," says a deep voice to my right. Oliver from Sociology is standing over our table. "Hey," he says to me. "Violet, it must have been weird for you in class today. I'm Oliver, by the way."

"Hi," I say. I usually know people's names before they know mine, but I'm glad I'm on equal name-footing with Oliver. I remembered his name because (a) it's unique enough and (b) I noticed that he wrote a smart Opinions column in the issue of the *Miscellany News*, Vassar's campus paper, that I picked up in the College Center last week.

"May I sit?" he asks, pulling up a chair before anyone answers.

Kurt snorts in disapproval, but Oliver ignores him. He's staring right at me. "So I know this might be weird—and Kurt's right that you don't owe anyone an explanation unless you want to offer one— but I'm wondering if you'd consider writing a piece for the newspaper about your experiences last year. Maybe something that gives us insight into this ad campaign you're a part of? I know everyone on campus is buzzing about you being here."

"They're what?" I ask, looking around the table at my suitemates and Kurt. "No one's said anything to me about—"

"It's the playing-it-cool factor," interrupts Kurt. "I told you that some people would do that."

I glance over at Jess. "Don't look at me," she says. "I truly had no idea you were like a famous model."

"I did," admits Fan, smiling sheepishly. "My best friend from home totally adored you and read your MySpace blog. But it's not like I was about to make you talk about things if you didn't feel like it. I also think you're just a pretty cool girl to share a suite with."

"You know me," says Kurt. "I was a screaming fan since day one when you rolled in with those glittering Louboutins."

"The glittering what?" asks Oliver, confused.

"Straight boys don't speak fashion," whispers Kurt, and I crack up.

I turn to Oliver. He's not unattractive with his close-cropped blond hair and warm brown eyes. He has a deep dimple that flashes on his left cheek when he smiles, and he looks like he would give a really solid hug. "Can I get back to you?" I ask. I'm not quite sure I want to draw more attention to the ad, but I am flattered that Oliver asked me to write something. Julie—who was editor in chief of our high school newspaper—would be jumping at this opportunity.

"Of course," says Oliver, standing up and pushing his chair back. "Let me know by Wednesday in class?"

"Okay," I say.

When Oliver leaves, Kurt raises his eyebrows at me.

"I don't know," I say, answering his implied *Do you really want to do this?* question. "It might be fun."

On Wednesday, I tell Oliver that I'll write the Opinions story, with the caveat that it has to focus on the modeling world in general—not on me or the Mirabella campaign specifically. I may still be blogging on myspace.com/violetgreenfield, but I'm not about to write something personal that's going into actual print and being archived in the Vassar Library. No way. He reluctantly agrees, but I only have a day to finish it—he wants it to run in Friday's paper.

I blow off my reading—midterms aren't for a while anyway—and focus on the article. I write about how the pressure that society puts on models is just as bad as the pressure that models put on society, how it's a vicious cycle that the fashion industry *and* the public have to break together, how there's a lot of blame put on individual models and designers, but it's really a bigger cultural issue. I close with this paragraph:

What I really hope is that women, in their all-shapes-and-sizes glory, realize that each one of us is unique. So whether you're in front of the camera or at home looking in the mirror, remember not to criticize too harshly. Take care of your body—and take pride in loving what you've got.

I sign the piece *Violet Greenfield* and I spell-check it twice. Then I e-mail it to Oliver before I can chicken out.

On Friday, Kurt rushes into our suite at ten a.m. I'm still sleeping, but Kurt has Intro to Art History on Friday mornings so he's always up. He bounds into my room and shakes my bed.

"Violet! Lookee what I have!"

I open my eyes halfway.

"It's not *Vogue*," he says, laughing. "It's the *Misc*."

The *Miscellany News*—my article is out.

I sit up in bed and grab the paper. My story's touted on the front page's Inside teaser, and it's published on page four. I flip to it and see a runway photo of myself from last year's Fashion Week—damn that style.com! Oh well—I guess the photo is relevant. I glance over the text and see that Oliver hasn't changed much, and he didn't really cut anything either.

"Did you read it?" I ask Kurt, looking up slowly.

"G-E-N-I-U-S!" he spells. "You are like the new star of campus. Everyone down in the College Center was talking about what a great piece it was. Seriously. It was like each time I turned a corner, someone else had the paper open to page four. I love it."

Fan bursts into my room with another copy of the paper.

"Violet Greenfield is the new Maureen Dowd," she says. "And when is your next column coming out? You know, the one about saving the planet from butylated hydroxytoluene."

Fan has gotten me really thinking about this green products thing. She sent me to teensforsafecosmetics.org and talked to me about how—if I do keep modeling and writing—I could really make a statement by wearing only green products. She even showed me these adorable and earth-friendly Earnest Sewn flats she got at Barneys, where they're apparently really into the green movement. I have to admit it's pretty cool. I even write a blog entry on myspace.com/violetgreenfield to tell my friends how much I respect the campaign, which I'm totally joining.

"Butty—what?" asks Kurt. "Fan, leave Violet alone—one cause per supermodel is quite enough."

"I think I can handle a couple," I say, smiling. It feels nice to be talked about for a positive reason, so why is my heart racing a little? I'm putting myself back in the spotlight, and I'm not totally sure I want to be there.

six

      If I was under the impression that people on campus didn't know I was a model, I can consider that illusion shattered after this weekend. I can't walk down to the Retreat without someone stopping me and telling me how much they liked the *Misc* article. I went to a dorm party in Cushing House this weekend and got totally cornered by a lovely group of lesbian model sympathizers at the keg. It's a little overwhelming, but it's better to be known for something good than something bad. And, as I remember from my years of being invisible in high school, it's no fun to be completely ignored.

    Kurt seems to be of that opinion too, I think, as I watch him take off his shirt and helicopter it over his head to get my attention in ACDC. I haven't even gotten over to the table when he booms, "Well, I never thought I'd have the pleasure of dining with a *New York Herald* writer! At least not until I manage to become Mr. Anderson Cooper!"

I laugh. "What are you talking about?" I ask, shaking my carton of orange juice.

"You didn't see?!" Kurt whips a newspaper out of his bag.

I roll my eyes and grab the paper, which is folded open to the Opinions page. "They excerpted my article!" I gasp. I'm not sure whether to be excited, angry, proud, or embarrassed. I look around the dining hall and spot Oliver sitting with the newspaper kids. I head straight for him.

He stands up before I get to the table. "Hey, Violet," he says. "Everyone's been wanting to meet you. This is Nicole, Joe, Nika, Kenn—"

"Hi!" I interrupt Oliver's list of names with a big wave addressed to everyone. Is he really planning to introduce me to all of the fourteen people sitting at his giant table? I have no time for that! "Um, Oliver, can I talk to you?"

"Sure," he says, smiling back at his friends. I grab his arm and pull him into a corner by a potted tree.

"What is this?" I ask, handing him the *Herald*. "And don't say 'a newspaper'—you know what I mean."

"You're not beyond thrilled that a real paper picked up your story?" he asks. "I thought you'd be—"

"I *am* thrilled!" I say angrily. "I mean, I don't know if I'm thrilled or not, and that's not the point. My question is: how did this get in here? I didn't give anyone permission."

"Well, this *Herald* editor kept calling you but couldn't get hold of you over the weekend," says Oliver. "So I told him that as your editor at the *Misc*, I was authorized to give him permission to run it."

"No one was calling me—" I start. But then I remember the missed 212 numbers that I assumed were from Angela trying to track me down by using a different phone line at Tryst. I look down at the paper. "A Model Viewpoint, by Violet Greenfield." It just ran today.

"I'm sorry," says Oliver. "I honestly thought you'd be really happy."

"It's okay," I say, realizing I actually *should* be excited about the article. *I wonder if Roger saw it*, I think, walking distractedly back to my table to sit down with Kurt.

"This is a good thing, right?" says Kurt hopefully when I return to my chair.

"I think so," I say.

Julie calls me that night. She's way excited, says that she's incredibly proud of me, and so on, but I can tell that she's also oozing jealous vibes. Being published in a real newspaper makes her more envious than any modeling accomplishments I've had. Journalism is like her life. She's an assistant features editor on Brown's school paper now, but she hasn't written anything for the outside world yet. I can't believe I beat her to it.

Roger doesn't get in touch until Wednesday. Not that I've been counting days, but it's just that he's usually so on top of things that I've been sort of looking for his Caller ID to pop up since my name appeared in the *Herald*. The Bravery's "Time Won't Let Me Go" signals his call.

"Hi," I say giddily. I actually sound giddy when I answer the phone. D'oh! Well, I haven't talked to him for a while, so that's why. It is *not* because I may love him. No way.

"I hate myself when I fall behind in my *Herald* reading!" he shouts. "You are a brilliant goddess of words. A complete and total rock star, V. Sincerely."

"You think?" I'm being coy. "Nah . . ."

"It's not an opinion," declares Roger. "It's a fact. So when are you coming down to be on the *Today* show? Will you think less of me if

I hold a poster that says 'I love Violet Greenfield' outside the window?"

My heart drops. *Is he kidding?*

"Just kidding." He laughs.

Oh. I collect my heart from my feet.

"But seriously, are you coming to the city anytime soon?" Roger asks.

"Um, I don't know," I say. "I mean, Veronica invited me to a party on Friday night, so I thought maybe—"

"Is it the *Teen Fashionista* Twenty-five Under Twenty-five party?" asks Roger. "Chloe's helping host with the other editors. I think Veronica's on the list this year, so I'm sure that's the one."

Chloe? Great. "Well, I mean, I'm not sure I can make it," I say. "I have a lot of work and—"

"Didn't you tell me you don't have Friday classes?" asks Roger.

"Well, I don't, but—" I stammer.

"That's my girl!" says Roger. "So we'll see you then. You know, they asked me to be on the list, too, but I thought, *Nah, let's leave the glory to the other young stars of today.*"

"Ha-ha," I say. But what I'm thinking is, *I'm not your girl. Chloe is. And what is all this* "We'll *see you*" *business. RoChloe is a "we"?*

When we hang up, I've somehow agreed to go to the city this weekend. Yikes.

I brought a ton of books on the Metro North train from Poughkeepsie to Grand Central, hoping I'd get some homework done during the two-hour ride. Do people in college still call it homework? I don't think they do, but that's what it is. Anyway, as I'm trying to read *The McDonaldization of Society 5*, I keep zoning out and staring at the Hudson River rolling past the window. This is a really beautiful ride. I sent Roger my train schedule info, just so he'd know when I was getting in. Okay, I'm half hoping he'll meet me at Grand Central, but I know that's silly. He's busy. He has, like, a real life in New York. And a real girlfriend.

I lean back onto the blue-and-maroon vinyl seats and grab my iPod, promising myself I'll just take a short break from reading. I set it to shuffle, and the first song that comes on is "I Want It That Way" by the Backstreet Boys. I always play it off as a joke if anyone else sees that Nick Carter and the boys are still on my iPod, but the truth is that I love this song. And it's the song that Roger and I sang to each other last year on the train from Madrid to Barcelona. That was on the night he kissed me. Was that really just a few months ago?

I let out an audible sigh as I sink farther into the seat. It's like fate that this song came on. I mean, I'm on a train—which isn't a normal thing for me—and I'm going to see Roger. It's like the iPod is psychic about what I want to hear—it just *knows*.

I get no reading done. I listen to music for the rest of the ride and I wonder why I blew off that kiss last year. In this moment, I'm not sure I regret anything more. Of course, I'm listening to the selection of love songs—Colbie Caillat's "Bubbly," Rihanna and Ne-Yo's "Hate That I Love You," and an oldie, "London Rain" by Heather Nova— that my iPod is cleverly shuffling for me. It knows me too well.

When we stop at Grand Central Station, I grab my bag and lug it off the train. I let myself get way too nostalgic on that ride. Even as I'm walking down the platform, I swear I see a familiar profile leaning against the doorway into the station. Navy blue hoodie, black-frame glasses, a torn-up paperback in his hands.

"Roger!" I shout, a little too enthusiastically as I drop my bag to give him a hug. He smirks and opens his arms.

"Miss Greenfield," he says, squeezing me. "What's up, Vassar girl?"

"You love saying that." I laugh.

"I read a Hemingway play once where the main character kept referring to his love interest as a 'Vassar Girl,'" he says. "And it's a classic label, right? Almost befitting a supermodel."

"I didn't even know Hemingway wrote plays, dork," I say.

"Ooh, then maybe you haven't quite earned the title yet." He smiles. "Come on, let's go."

"Where are we going?" I ask.

"My dorm," says Roger. "We'll drop your stuff off and hang out. That's why you sent me your train schedule, isn't it? So I'd pick you up?"

"It was just FYI," I say nonchalantly. "I mean, I figured if you had nothing to do . . ."

"Oh, okay," says Roger, rolling his eyes. "Listen, I know you need red-carpet treatment. Besides, this is my town now."

As we walk under the glowing blue zodiac-covered ceiling of the train station, he holds out his elbow for me to link my arm through. "That and I didn't have Friday classes and I was totally bored."

I laugh and squeeze his arm—*whoa*. Has he been working out?

When we reach his dorm Roger is bouncing up and down on his left leg, his classic pee dance since we were little kids. "Gotta pee!" he shouts as he bounds out of the elevator.

"Go, go!" I say as he turns around and throws me the keys to his room. "Third door on the left!" he shouts again.

I actually would have remembered exactly where it was. I was here last year, the night I flew back from Paris. Chloe was here too.

Right now, though, it's just me and Roger, I remind myself as I open the door. At least for a few hours.

But when I walk inside the room, I see that Chloe is more pervasive than I gave her credit for. There are fresh flowers on the dresser—which is so not something Roger would have on his own—and I count nine (*nine!*) photos of RoChloe, plus two of just Chloe alone. One is obviously from a professional photo shoot—probably some *Teen Fashionista* "Meet the Assistants" page, but Chloe does look decent. Oh, who am I kidding? She has these bouncy blond curls and a cute spray of freckles. Plus she's got blue eyes and perfect little pink lips. Who cares if she's not a size 2? She's pretty! I just don't want to admit it.

When Roger walks into the room, I'm holding up a framed picture of Chloe. I jump and put it down clumsily, knocking it over. "Oops!" I say, turning red. Roger doesn't seem to notice, though. He's bounding toward me to set it upright. "Isn't that one adorable?" he says, beaming.

"Yeah," I say, fighting my gag reflex.

"She was on set one day for a fashion story and the photographer just thought she was too pretty not to shoot," he says, still staring at the photo.

Does he really like her this much?

"So," I say, clapping my hands to snap Roger out of his Chloe-worshipping mode. "What are we gonna do today?"

First, we go out to lunch at a vegetarian place Roger says everyone loves. "Are you a vegetarian now?" I ask, eyebrow raised.

"Chloe is," he says. "And I know we used to think that was lame, but she's not one of those annoying types who dictates the restaurant."

"Um, is that why we're currently dining at a meatless establishment even though she's not even here?" I ask, using my best sarcastic voice.

"Shut up," says Roger, laughing. "It's good!"

And he's right. It is good. *For a vegetarian place.*

When we finish, we walk down the street to Roger's favorite coffee shop. He has this plan to take me to all the places he loves around NYU. Our breath comes out in clouds as we take in the cold air. We get to the hipster-filled joint, and I order an iced coffee. When the guy behind the counter looks at me funny, Roger jumps in.

"Winter or not, she must have a cold drink," he says. "Hot drinks make her feel like she's sick. That's because her mom gave her too much TheraFlu as a child."

I smile and nod. The guy behind the counter grumbles at having to ice a drink in winter. I get that a lot.

We sit down by a big window with our coffees and stare out at the people walking by in warm, bulky coats.

"Don't you love real winter?" asks Roger.

I think of the slushy rain that passed for snow in North Carolina.

"It's okay," I say, sliding the wrapper off my straw very carefully. "It'll improve if I get to make a snowman this year." I remove the wrapper in a perfectly accordion-folded line, and Roger sprinkles one drop of coffee on it so that it starts to move like a worm. I can't help myself—I giggle like I'm six years old.

"The straw worm is still a Violet pleaser," he says, smiling at me. His cheeks are pink from the cold outside, and that somehow makes his deep blue eyes sparkle more than usual. I feel myself getting flushed, but I know my cheeks are still cold-pink too, so he probably won't notice—I hope.

We sit there for hours, talking. We wonder what the halls of Chapel Hill High School are like without us ("Empty of wit," says

Roger); we discuss whether the guy at Katie's Pretzels has noticed we no longer come in for one cinnamon and one parmesan flavor twice a week (Roger thinks he definitely misses us); we briefly consider whether or not our coffee attendant would be called a *barist-o* since he's a guy; and we ponder Julie's well-being at Brown ("Do you think she has time to eat between all her extracurriculars and completely overloaded class schedule?").

After we've each had two refills, a guy in black-and-white-striped shirt and a beret walks in carrying his own bar stool. Roger eyes him warily. "That guy looks suspiciously like a mime," he whispers.

"Or a really brave creative writing student," I say.

"Either way . . ." says Roger.

"We should get out of here before he starts—" I try to finish Roger's thought, but it's too late. The mime-poet is tapping the mike. So I guess that makes him not a mime.

"Hi," he says. "I'm Jeff and I have an original poem to read for you this evening."

Other people seem open to Jeff. They're quieting their conversations and turning in their chairs to look at him.

Roger and I lock eyes and then we get up and bolt for the door simultaneously. We burst onto the street, trying not to crack up until the door closes behind us and we've run out of sight of the window.

"That would have been intolerable!" shouts Roger through choked laughter.

"No way," I say. "As soon as that guy walked in I smelled an open-mike night. I thought you said that was your favorite café!"

"I never go there past seven p.m.," says Roger. "I had no idea it had that kind of evening scene."

"Is it past seven?" I ask, grabbing Roger's arm to look at the charmingly worn watch his grandfather gave him in ninth grade. "We're late!"

We both start running back to Roger's dorm, half laughing, half gasping for air as we reach the elevator.

"How long do you think it'll take you to get ready?" asks Roger.

"Three minutes," I say. "I'm good like that."

"I'm timing you," he says. "We were supposed to be there fifteen minutes ago."

"I bet I'm faster than you," I say.

"Game on!" Roger shouts.

When the elevator dings open, we race to his door. It's open, and Roger's roommate is lying in a lump on the second bed. I tiptoe in, but Roger says, "He's dead to the world," in full voice. "I swear," he affirms when I look at him doubtfully. "He sleeps through everything. Even when Chloe's over it's like he's just passed out cold."

Ew. My temporary bubble—the one where just Roger and I exist in the world—pops.

I grab my bag and head into the bathroom to throw on the very packable black-and-white Diane von Furstenberg dress I've got with me—it never wrinkles. My five-inch heels come in handy tonight—they add some color to my dress. Kurt made me promise to wear the Louboutins even though I told him I can barely walk in them. "Beauty is pain!" he declared dramatically. I told him he sounded like my agent.

I throw my hair up into a sloppy-chic bun, make my lips pop with my new favorite red lipstick, and swipe a blue-tinged mascara wand over my lashes. Done. I look good, but my shoulders slouch as I stare at myself in the full-length bathroom mirror. *Chloe the twenty-two-year-old sleeps over at the dorm. Gross.*

Suddenly the door bursts open and two girls rush in, laughing. They stop when they see me.

"Violet Greenfield?" says the first one. The second just stands there as her mouth falls open. "You're, like, on our hall."

"Yeah," I say, feeling totally awkward. "Hi." I wave stupidly. "I'm just visiting someone."

"Ooh, Rachel! Remember?" says the second girl to the first. "She's friends with Sterno!"

Sterno. Roger's college nickname is lame-o.

"Yup," I say, trying to edge past them as they stand in front of the door. "Sterno and I are high school friends. And we're late for—"

"Are you coming to the keg party later?" interrupts not-Rachel. "Everyone would be so excited if you showed."

"Um, I don't know if—"

Mercifully, Roger pushes open the bathroom door. "I thought you said you were fast," he says. "I'm already—" He stops when he sees Rachel and not-Rachel.

"Ladies," he says. "Are you harassing my oldest and dearest friend?"

"We're inviting her to tonight!" says Rachel. "Make sure she comes." Apparently I'm some sort of party trick.

"We've got our own schedule," says Roger. "But we'll see." He grabs my arm and pulls me out of the bathroom.

"Caught by rabid fans!" he says, when we get back to his room. "Sorry about that. Is it weird for you when people know who you are?"

"I guess," I say. "But it's not like I'm Gisele Bündchen or someone really famous. It doesn't happen that much."

Roger doesn't say anything, but he's looking at me. Then he lets out a sigh and shakes his head a little. "You look really pretty," he says.

"Thanks," I say. "You do too."

We smile at each other for a moment—one that feels kind of meaningful.

"That's what I was going for," he says. "Pretty."

"You know what I mean," I say, sorry that his fleeting sincerity is gone. But he does look really great in his black blazer and white button-down shirt.

"Better than prom?" Roger asks.

"Nothing could be better than prom," I say, remembering our date. Was that just last spring?

"Chloe picked out the jacket," says Roger, holding out the lapel to show me the blue silk inner lining. "She even took me to get it tailored. She says that clothes look more expensive if the fit is right."

Chloe, Chloe, Chloe! "You sound gay," I say. "Let's go."

seven

When we arrive at Marquee, Roger immediately gets in the press line. Two girls dressed in all black with clipboards and those weird head mikes are working the door. Their hair is slicked back into identical ponytails like those women in that old eighties video "Addicted to Love." They're checking off names.

"Chloe put us on the list," says Roger, bouncing up and down on his toes like he's so proud of Chloe for being so ultra-special. I roll my eyes behind his back. I look around and see a lot of women holding designer bags that have a waiting list and wearing David Yurman jewelry. The fact that I recognize these things scares me. I'm not sure I want to be here.

But then I recognize something else—and I see a way to outdo Chloe. "Charles?" I shout to the bouncer at the door. He smiles slowly. "Violet! Come on through," he says, waving and lifting the velvet rope for me and Roger. I guess last year's exploits were good for something. Eat that, press line!

"Smooth," whispers Roger as we enter the club. I smile, but my moment of triumph is short-lived. Chloe bounds over and practically knocks Roger down with her voracious hug. *Could she be more annoying?*

I avert my eyes as they canoodle and I see a fury of flashbulbs in the corner. There's a giant *Teen Fashionista* logo backdrop and a short red carpet where the press is gathered to take pictures of the big names who attend the party.

"That's the Twenty-five Under Twenty-five," says Chloe. "Veronica Trask is on the red carpet right now—they love her."

I push through the crowd to reach my old roommate, and I gasp when I see her. She's in head-to-toe liquid silver—a dress that drapes down to the floor with a deep V-neck that must require some major double-stick boob tape. Her sky-high cheekbones are catching the light and her dark brown hair swings as her bright pink lips go from full smile to sexy smirk to pouty frown. The girl knows how to work a photo shoot.

I suddenly feel underdressed.

"V!" I hear Veronica's happy shout before I feel the heat of twenty flashbulbs turning on me. She grabs my arm and helps me duck under the press ropes so I can join her on the red carpet. Yup, definitely underdressed. We squeeze each other's hands as we pose together—the things I've learned over the last year come back to me naturally. I instantly go into the thin angle: pivot one hip back, elbow out to the side, head tilted slightly.

After a couple minutes, I tug on Veronica's hand.

"Enough?" she whispers through her smile.

"Yes," I whisper back.

We leave the red carpet to a few protest shouts, but then Hayden Panettierre arrives, so the photographers quickly forget we exist.

"How are you?" Veronica asks as we find a dark corner to talk in. "I see you decided to come down and visit your true love." She gestures at Roger, who's still standing with Chloe. They're both laughing.

"He's her true love now," I say defeatedly.

"Please," says Veronica. "A too-old flavor of the moment could never top your history. Besides, you're hotter."

"Thanks," I say. "I feel a little casual for tonight, though—I didn't think I'd be making a press appearance."

"You look fantastic, as always," says Veronica. "Besides, in those heels you could wear a potato sack and make it fashion."

I smile. Kurt was right.

"I'm glad to see you, Veronica," I say. "I just am not really into the whole 'being photographed' thing right now."

"V, with the campaign out, we've got to do as much press as we can," says Veronica. She sounds annoyed with me.

"Are you mad at me?" I ask.

She sighs. "I'm not mad," she says. I feel a *but* coming. "It's just that we're in this Mirabella ad together and I'm pulling all the weight. It's like you're already retired or something. People are always asking me where you are, if you're working . . ."

"Well, tell them I'm in school," I say. "Don't people ever go to college in this industry?"

"Not while they're still on the rise," says Veronica. "It's like you're dropping out just when things could get really great for you."

But I already know this line—I've heard it from Angela. "No," I say. "It's not for me right now."

"Double V!" I hear a cheery Australian accent as I spin around to greet Sam, our old roommate.

"Group hug!" I shout, hoping Veronica will drop the issue now that Sam's here. Sam always lightens things up.

"You came into the city for the party?" asks Sam, smiling at me.

"She came into the city for a boy," says Veronica before I can answer. She's staring at Roger. He notices, and he and Chloe start toward us.

"What do you mean?" asks Sam. "Isn't that your friend Roger from high school?"

"I'll explain later!" I whisper hurriedly as RoChloe approaches.

"Hi, Roger," says Veronica, smiling in a way that makes me nervous. *Please don't let her say anything weird.*

"Veronica," he says, kissing her cheek. What a New York party thing to do. How did Roger learn that?

"Hi, ladies!" gushes Chloe, leaning in to kiss both Veronica and Sam on the cheeks.

Before we can launch into awkward conversation, I hear a commanding voice from across the room.

"Chloe!" shouts an elegant gray-haired woman to our left. She's holding up her arm as if to summon a servant. She's wearing a short black dress with large rosettes at the hem, and a ginormous diamond cocktail ring flashes on her pinky. She radiates chic.

"Who's that?" I whisper, to no one in particular.

"Marilyn Flynn," says Sam out of the corner of her mouth. "The editor in chief of *Teen Fashionista.*"

"And Chloe's boss," adds Roger. Chloe has rushed to Marilyn Flynn's side and is nodding rapidly. I strain to hear them.

"There's trouble by the DJ booth," says Marilyn Flynn. "I told you to watch Valentina around the champagne. She's trying to take over the music. Beauty editors are so outlandish. Grab her!"

Marilyn Flynn waves her arm dismissively and Chloe is off like a shot, trying to break up a scuffle between the DJ and the beauty editor.

Then Marilyn Flynn sets her sights on our group. She steps into the circle. "Roy." She nods at Roger in greeting and he just smiles, not correcting her. Then he subtly slips away, like he knows this isn't his world. I watch him walk over toward the bar, and I wish I could join him.

"Veronica, you look stunning," says Marilyn Flynn.

"Thank you, Marilyn," murmurs Veronica. Sometimes she can be so genteel. "You know Sam, of course."

"Yes, darling," says Marilyn Flynn. "Swimsuits last summer." Sam smiles. She always does swimsuit shots, which is why she spends half her time in Florida. I know she wishes she could move into other markets.

"And this is Violet Greenfield," says Veronica, gesturing at me.

"Hello," I say, not sure whether to hold out my hand or lean in for a party kiss or what. You'd think I'd know these things by now, but Marilyn Flynn doesn't move. I think she's a non-toucher.

"Of course I know Violet," she says. "Chloe profiled her last summer in a lovely piece. I've been dying to meet you, dear."

"Oh, thanks," I say. Then a long silence falls.

The way Marilyn Flynn is looking at me makes me nervous, like I don't know where to put my hands or how to stand, so I grab a crab cake from a passing waiter. But then it's like, *I'm holding a crab cake with white sauce on top*, so I pop it into my mouth and focus on chewing daintily, which—if you've ever tried—is impossible. Chewing is not dainty. Just as my mouth is full of crab, Marilyn opens hers.

"So, Violet, I hear you're at Vassar," she says.

I work my jaw voraciously, trying to clear my mouth as I nod at her and attempt a smile.

"I've always loved that campus," she continues. "Such lovely trees and gorgeous architecture."

Almost done with crab. Keep smiling. Chew, chew, chew. Swallow!

"Is your schedule very hectic?" Marilyn Flynn asks.

"It's challenging but not overly stressful," I say, praying there are no food remnants in my teeth while I give her the answer my parents seem to like.

"Her Fridays are free," says Veronica, smiling at Marilyn Flynn. "So she can do bookings then."

I look over at Veronica questioningly, and she winks. *Why is she trying to start something?*

"I was thinking less of bookings and more of an internship," says Marilyn Flynn.

"At *Teen Fashionista*?" I ask, stupidly. *No, at* Newsweek. *Duh!*

"Of course," smiles Marilyn, showing her pearly whites. "An editorial internship. I read your piece in the *Herald*."

I look over to where Roger is still standing and trying to get a drink. I so want him to hear this conversation—I'm being intellectually appreciated here! Someone wants me for something other than my height and weight!

"Say yes, Violet," purrs Marilyn Flynn. "I've always wanted to have a model intern."

My heart sinks. But just a little bit. Even if she does want me because I've walked a runway, she's also noticed my writing. I can prove that I'd be a great asset to *Teen Fashionista*. Maybe I can write about body image—or about how going green is this huge new thing in the fashion and beauty industry (Fan would *love* me for that).

"That sounds great," I say.

"Fabulous," says Marilyn Flynn. Then she claps her hands in the air. "Chloe!" she shouts.

Chloe comes running over from the now-pacified situation at the DJ booth. "Yes, Marilyn?" she asks obediently. Roger made it seem like Chloe ran the magazine, but I'm evilly satisfied to see her in this subservient role.

"Violet's going to start interning at *Teen Fashionista*," Marilyn Flynn says. "You'll be in charge of her."

I will my eyes not to roll.

"Great!" says Chloe, grinning doofily at me.

I can't read this girl. She could be like, "Great!" in her bubbly way and be truly excited. Or she may mean, "Great! Because I'm going to enjoy being a complete bitch to her in addition to stealing her best-friend-slash-true-love!"

I smile at Chloe as Marilyn Flynn excuses herself to chat with what is surely a more important group of people.

"This will be fun!" Chloe chirps when Marilyn's gone.

I squeak out a meek, "Yeah," and grab Veronica and Sam, pulling them to the bar. "Excuse us," I say to Chloe.

When I'm out of earshot, I start whining. "What did I just do?" I ask them.

"Babe, you just took an internship at a great magazine," says Sam. "An *editorial* internship—you'll probably get to write something for them!"

"But working under *Chloe*?" I look over at Veronica, who understands this Roger-Chloe-Me triangle infinitely better than Sam does. Truth be told, Sam is sort of out of the loop.

"Violet, have I ever told you what my mother said to me when I left for New York to start my modeling career?" Veronica asks, eyes shining.

"No," I say, curious. I've never heard a peep about Veronica's mom.

"Keep your friends close, and your enemies closer," she says.

I look over at Chloe, who's huddled in the corner with Roger.

"Your mother is a smart lady," I say.

eight

The next Friday, I'm on my way back to the city—this time I had to catch the seven twenty-six a.m. Metro North train. I'm so tired that I again abandon my reading to lean against the window and let my eyelids get heavy. This hour of the morning should be imposed exclusively on people over thirty—or people with dogs. *Ugh*.

I called my parents to tell them about the *Teen Fashionista* internship, and they seemed happy for me, though it was clear they didn't really know much about the magazine beyond the one issue we have on our coffee table (and that's because I'm featured in it). Jake cleared thirty seconds from his schedule to say "That's cool. Congratulations," and then to tell me that the basketball team is "kicking some serious ass" this year, which felt like a bonding moment.

But it's my friends up here who are really into my news. When I told Kurt about the internship, he screamed. "That is only my favorite magazine right now!" he shouted. "Well, my favorite non-dirty, non-*Vogue* mag anyway. What is Marilyn Flynn like? Did you meet any fashion editors? Can I come see the offices?"

I had to tell him to slow down, but he wouldn't stop harassing me until I promised to take a photo of the famed shoe closet. "I need it for MySpace," he said. Jess and Fan were psyched for me too, until they realized I wouldn't be able to party on Thursday nights anymore this semester. I went to bed at midnight last night and I'm still exhausted. Maybe that's because even though I went to bed at midnight, I couldn't fall asleep, so I wandered out into the common room and played Mexicali with my suitemates until two a.m. Maybe that's also why I have this killer headache.

I pop an Advil when I get to Grand Central, and then I walk a few long blocks to face the glass doors of Bruton Publications, where the *Teen Fashionista* offices are on the fourteenth floor. Immediately, I'm a little overwhelmed by the people around me. A flurry of women in high heels, stylish sundresses, and tailored designer shirts rush by as they swipe their ID cards past the guards and head for the elevator banks. I stand in the entrance for a moment, wondering if I've accidentally stumbled into a Fashion Week tent instead of an office building.

My name is on the approved visitor list, so I'm allowed into the hallowed halls of Bruton. On the fourteenth floor, there's a blond receptionist with a headset on. "Help you?" she asks, not looking up from her computer. She has a really strong New York accent and she's wearing a ton of foundation, which doesn't quite cover the freckles I suspect she's trying to hide.

"Um, I'm Violet Greenfield," I say. "Here to start my internship."

She looks up and smacks her gum. "It *is* you, huh?" She gives me a half smile. "I saw your name on the log this morning, but I thought it'd be some other Greenfield. Shoulda known Marilyn would bring in supermodel interns one day."

"Oh, I'm not—" I start.

"Don't be modest around here, honey," she says, leaning forward as if to take me into her confidence. "Anything that gets these bitches' respect? Milk it."

I laugh nervously as she picks up her phone. "Chloe? Your new intern's here."

An hour later, I'm sitting on the floor in a closet filled with products. Beauty products, that is. There's a cheek shelf, two lips shelves, four eye shelves and various other categorizations of what seems like every bit of makeup on the planet. There's a special shelf for things from Sephora, and a whole 'nother section for designer merchandise from places like Chanel and Dior. My job is to clear some of the many bags from the floor and organize the products on the shelves. Chloe dropped me off here about half an hour ago, after perfunctorily introducing me to another editorial assistant, a features editor, and Valentina, the beauty editor from the party last week (who promptly recruited me for this first task). I guess I was a little naïve about what I'd be doing at the magazine as an intern. So much for writing.

I can't be sure, but I think I detected a little smile on Chloe's lips as she left me in this stuffy closet with what seems like a thousand bags. "Take lunch between noon and one," she told me. Then she added, "Don't forget to have fun!" in her singularly annoying twitter-voice before closing the door on me.

Just last summer, I was surrounded by bags like these in a totally different setting. My first day in Brazil before I walked the shows in São Paulo, I was greeted at my hotel by prettily wrapped gifts with tissue paper spilling out of the tops. But these aren't gifts for me— they're for *Teen Fashionista*—and I'm not a runway model anymore.

I'm an intern. The bottom of the totem pole. This is what I wanted . . . right?

As I'm placing the twelfth mascara wand on the shelf, I hear a knock at the door. Valentina enters with a tall, regal-looking girl who's got an upturned nose and a perfectly shiny brown bob. "Meet Alexia," says Valentina. "She's our beauty intern, and she'll be taking over the closet now."

"Hi, I'm Violet," I say, smiling at Alexia even though she totally scares me. I'm using Veronica's first rule of interacting with potentially difficult people: *Do Not Show Fear.*

"I know," she says, brushing past me to get at the bags. Valentina shuts the door and leaves us without another word.

"So I was just putting the mascara here and—" I start.

"I've got it," she interrupts, with a tone that moves her category from *potentially difficult* to *definite a-hole* in my mind.

"Okay, well I'll help you—" I try again.

"Listen, Miss Model," she snips, turning her back on me to re-arrange some of the products I've already organized. "Why don't you run along and see if the fashion department needs someone to file shoes for them or something? Beauty is *mine*."

I throw up my hands behind her back in frustration. *What is with this girl?* But although I can be passive-aggressive, I'm so not into confrontation. I turn and quietly walk out of the closet.

I find Chloe's desk through the maze of cubicles, but she's not there so I linger near her cube. I'm really not sure what to do with myself now that I don't have a task. Then I see Marilyn Flynn coming down the hall toward me. She has two assistants with clipboards walking behind her, taking notes on whatever it is that she's rapidly saying.

"And I want there to be peonies—more than we've ever used before. Fill the room if you have to but get me hundreds of blooms. We need—"

I'm trying to slink halfway into Chloe's cube. Not so far that she thinks I'm invading her private space while she's not around, but enough so that I'm not visible in the hallway. I don't want Marilyn Flynn to notice me. When I hear her stop midsentence, though, I know I've been spotted.

"Violet, dear," she says, changing her tone from authoritative boss lady to warm Auntie Marilyn. "How is your first day?"

"Oh, good," I say. "I was just helping out in the beauty closet and now I'm waiting for—"

"Beauty closet?" she asks. "What imbecile stuffed you in there?"

"Well, Chloe said that Valentina needed help with—"

"You should be doing story research, not alphabetizing lipstick!" roars Marilyn. "Chlo-eee!" Her shriek echoes across the office and I hear a panting Chloe run from down the hall.

"Yes, Marilyn?" she asks, appearing at her boss's side.

"Set Violet up with a desk," says Marilyn. "Get her a login and an e-mail and don't let me hear about her working the beauty closet again."

"Yes, Marilyn," says Chloe.

When Marilyn's high-heeled bootsteps have disappeared down to her office, Chloe looks over at me.

"Guess you're the new favorite," she says, smiling.

I shrug innocently. *Why do I have the feeling that's not going to win me any friends around here?*

Later that day, my cubicle is set up (right next to Chloe's) and I have my very own e-mail account. I see Alexia strut by, her swingy bob shining in the fluorescent lights, but she doesn't turn to say hello. In fact, I think she sped up when she got near my desk.

Chloe puts me to work on a diet story—I'm supposed to research how sodas and sugary drinks like coffee frappuccinos can have as many calories as a huge dessert. So I'm basically Googling "calories, can of Coke" and then "calories, Krispy Kreme" for comparison's sake. It's not rocket science, but it's fun to think that my research will help inform a real story in the magazine.

I'm trying to type all my data into a neat document before I leave to meet Roger tonight, but it's four p.m. and my mind is wandering. Chloe has to go to an event where she doesn't have a "plus one" invite, so Roger asked if I wanted to see a movie. All day I've been wondering if Chloe knows I'm going to hang out with Roger later. She hasn't mentioned it. Is it weird if she doesn't know? Either way, I'm excited.

Then, for the first time, my desk phone rings. "*Teen Fashionista*," I answer, mimicking what I've heard Chloe saying.

"Volatile Violet," says the all-knowing voice on the other end.

"Hi, Angela," I say. I guess dodging my robo-agent's calls to my cell and not answering her MySpace messages didn't deter her.

"I assume you're quite the Vassar girl now," she purrs.

She doesn't even sound mad that I haven't gotten in touch since I left Paris in November. But then she keeps talking.

"I am a little miffed at you, darling. Why didn't you tell me you were working at *Teen Fashionista*? Why did I have to read about it in *Women's Wear Daily*'s roundup of high-profile interns?"

Ugh. The fact that there even is such a roundup—and that I would actually be on it—makes me feel queasy. But before I can express dismay, I realize Angela isn't done talking.

"And then I had to track you down through some sort of Bruton switchboard like a person who can't even get a direct line for an intern. Humiliating. Of course I told everyone who asked that I arranged the whole thing, so let's stick with that story when we talk to people, shall we?"

"Uh, okay," I say, using the unsure tone I often have when talking to my agent. Actually, I'm not even positive she's my agent anymore since I haven't done a modeling job in months. And I'm not planning to.

"So when can we get you back to work?" she asks. "I was thinking some go-sees for the shows this month, and then maybe we'll have a shot at landing another fabulous campaign. You know, the Mirabella ads are causing quite a stir. Always controversial, aren't you, Violet?"

"What do you mean?" I ask.

"Well, your piece in the *Herald*, all the bloggers going on and on about the significance of your svelte figure next to a Love Your Body message," she says. "I'm fielding an awful lot of calls for you. Of course, I'll guard you from that nasty media machine."

This is what I was afraid of when I left the campaign. I knew it. A high-fashion ad starring me wouldn't be the right venue for a positive body image statement. I just wanted to do something good, but I'm afraid it backfired. I've been trying to live my life offline and I've really tuned out of answering my phone, so I haven't heard much beyond Vassar's walls. But now as I bring up a new browser window and Google my name, I feel faint. There are more than two hundred thousand entries, and I can tell by the first ten that not all of them are fan clubs. I scan the word *hypocrite* seven times.

"Thanks," I say to Angela, grateful for her gatekeeping ways, which I used to think were annoying.

"Not a problem, darling," Angela coos. "Now how about those go-sees? Are you ready to walk?"

"Um, can we talk next week?" I ask, not ready to tell her no, but also trying hard not to commit to yes.

"I'll call you Monday, Vexing Violet," she says, sounding a little ominous. "Remember, you're still under contract with Tryst."

And then she's gone, leaving me sighing into a dial tone. I'll never get used to her lack of good-bye etiquette.

I close the search window, not wanting to read more than the dozen-word summaries of the hits my name turned up. If I need evidence that it's time to leave the modeling world for good, I think I just got it. So why couldn't I tell Angela no? Maybe it's because I'm afraid of her, or maybe it's because I don't know how to get out of something so official as the contract I have with Tryst. Or maybe it's because I'm still not sure who I am or what I have to offer if I'm not modeling's next big thing. But I'd like to find out.

nine

When I leave the *Teen Fashionista* offices that night, I decide to stop by the beauty closet and wish Alexia a good weekend. Maybe if I make an effort she won't scare me so much. As I approach the door, I hear muffled voices and a scrap of conversation. I don't catch all of it, but what I hear is enough: "Can't believe she was on a runway just this fall . . . campaign retouching . . . chipmunk cheeks." Alexia is talking some major shit—about me. I pause at the door, half wanting to bolt, half wanting to hear more. A year ago, I would definitely have just walked away, but now the part of me that wants to run is overruled. I open the door swiftly, plastering a smile across my face.

"Hi, Alexia!" I say cheerfully. "Just wanted to wish you a great weekend!"

She turns, cell phone to her ear, and gives me a grin with way too much teeth-and-gum action. "Ta, Violet." Then she waves dismissively and slams the door.

I walk down the hallway to the elevator. Maybe she wasn't talking about me, I think. Maybe someone they just shot for a beauty story had puffy cheeks. Maybe the campaign she mentioned isn't Mirabella.

But as I reach the lobby, I can feel my shoulders slouching already. I wonder if I'll ever fit in somewhere, just naturally. I almost call Roger to cancel our movie night, but then I realize there's nothing I need more than to sit next to my best friend in a dark theater. It's a safe place for me. Plus, I really want some movie popcorn.

When I get there, Roger already has our tickets. He gets very antsy about seat selection, so I tell him to find us a spot while I order a number three combo—large popcorn, two medium sodas, and a pack of Twizzlers. Whenever I'm at a movie theater, I feel this weird sense of community with the workers there. I guess it's because I worked at the Palace Theater in Chapel Hill for two years. I hear the woman next to me complaining about the cost of a large drink—and I don't blame her, it's way overpriced—but I also know that if you're the person on the other side of the register in a vest and bow tie, you hear that gripe about twenty times a day and it's not like you've got anything to do with it. I smile at the girl behind the counter, hoping to convey that I understand, that I too have had to handle these kinds of people.

I sit down next to Roger and compliment him on the perfect seat choice. He got us into the row behind the wheelchair spot so there's total leg room, which I appreciate. I open the Twizzlers immediately and bite a bit of both ends off one.

"Candy straw," says Roger. He taught me this trick in third grade.

"Mmm . . ." I murmur, already sipping my Diet Sprite.

The lights dim slightly and previews start. One thing I love about going to a movie with Roger is that we never have to speak.

With some people, you have to acknowledge each preview as it plays: "Oh, this looks good," or "I'll pass on that one." When it's me and Roger, we both know what the other's opinion on a coming attraction is, and we also just want to watch and lose ourselves in the screen. It's this unspoken vibe. But then he breaks it.

"Hey," he whispers after the last preview. "Thanks for being my date tonight."

"Anytime," I say, smiling at him in the dark. And then I settle down into my chair, really glad I didn't cancel.

After the movie, we go to a coffee shop around the corner. I promised Kurt I'd come back to campus tonight—he has this theory that the more I'm gone from Vassar, the less of a social life I'll have there. I see his point, but I want just one more hour with Roger.

"You seem kinda down," he says to me as we claim our window seat.

"I guess I am," I say.

"Is the magazine work hard to do with school and all?" he asks.

"No, that's not it," I say. I cross my legs and stare out the window, wondering what to say to Roger. I know he doesn't like it when I talk about the modeling world. It's like this part of me he doesn't want to know.

"Angela called me today," I say, deciding to just go for it. If I can't talk to Roger about something, it's almost like it isn't real. "She wants to know when I can go back to work."

"But I thought you said you quit," he says. I sense a note of judgment in his tone.

"I did," I say. "But it's not just something I can say to her. I have a contract or whatever, I think."

"You think?" asks Roger. "Violet, that's a detail you should be aware of."

"I know, but it just seemed so complicated," I say, remembering when I signed the papers last summer to extend my time with Tryst. I didn't even really think about it. "My mom took care of things," I explain.

"Well, then I'd give her a call and figure out what the deal is," says Roger, shaking his head like he can't believe this conversation.

But this isn't even what I really want to talk about, I realize. It's not like I need to rehash the details of my contract with Roger. I look down at my nails and start picking at the thin skin around my thumb.

"Someone said I was fat today at work," I say.

"What?!" Roger says, rolling his eyes. "They were obviously joking. You're like the opposite of fat."

"She wasn't joking," I say. "She said I had chipmunk cheeks and she couldn't believe I was on a runway last fall."

"Are we seriously giving air time to this girl's comments?" Roger asks. "She's clearly jealous."

"Maybe," I say, considering the possibility. Marilyn Flynn has given me much better jobs than Alexia gets at the magazine. "But I have gained some weight since last fall and—"

"I'm sorry," Roger interrupts. "I just can't listen to another insecure model rant. Can we change the subject?"

"What do you mean by that?" I ask.

"I'm tired of it, Violet," he says. "It's weird when you talk about your size that way—you're really thin, and whining about being fat is incredibly lame."

"You don't get it," I say, standing up.

"Don't get what?" he asks, confused.

It's about how I've never been able to fit in anywhere. Not in high school, not in the modeling world, not at this new internship. It's like I'm a mean-girl magnet, and I'm starting to wonder if it's something about me that's the problem.

But I don't say any of that. I just stare at him. Roger rolls his eyes and looks out the window. "What is the problem, Violet?" he asks, exasperated.

"Forget it," I say, picking up my bag. I walk out of the café and head for the subway. I know at least one place where it feels like I'm starting to fit in: I'm going back to Vassar.

The minute I get to campus, I feel like a weight is lifted off me. I take a cab from the train station to my dorm, where there's a huge party going on in the College Center. I push through the crowds of people in bras and body glitter to find Kurt, Fan, and Jess by the glowing green punch bowl.

"Violet!!" shrieks Kurt, attracting way too much attention. "What the hell are you wearing?!" He pulls my arm and drags me toward the stairs.

"Kurt!" I protest.

"Honey, you've got to get out of these office-appropriate clothes," he says, shaking his head. "This is no way for a supermodel to dress at an all-campus party."

When we return to Fan and Jess, who haven't moved from their perch near the punch, I'm wearing a gold-and-silver-sequined mini-dress that Sam made me buy in Paris last year. It's pretty fabulous, I have to admit, but I feel like it draws too many stares.

"You guys don't think this is too, 'Oh, I'm a model and I bought this in Paris last season'?" I ask Fan and Jess.

"Please, Violet!" shouts Kurt over the pumping house music. "That's the vibe you *want* to give off. Show your stuff, Miss Diva."

I laugh and plunge a cup into the punch, realizing that Kurt is really good at helping me get over myself.

When we get back to the suite for our own personal after-party, the four of us congregate around Jess's laptop to watch a video Kurt wants us to see on funnyordie.com. It's these guys singing about how they worship Will Ferrell. We watch it three times before I close the window, and Kurt is still humming.

"Oh, Violet, I friended you on MySpace," says Fan.

"Cool," I say. I haven't checked my page in a while. It sort of scares me because sometimes people leave harsh comments or the press will pick up things I post and use it on gossip blogs. But I open up my page to accept Fan anyway. It's lame to be afraid of a website.

Fan, Jess, and Kurt start playing a round of Mexicali with the Busch Light we have left in our mini-fridge, but I don't join in. I'm sucked into the comments and messages on myspace.com/violet greenfield. There are actually a lot of really supportive people sending stuff to me. Girls who say that they love the Mirabella ad, that they're happy to see the healthy body focus. And then there are the haters ("Don't try to preach about body image, you skinny bitch!"). I guess I shouldn't be surprised.

I do notice one message in particular. It's from a health teacher in Brooklyn who wants to know if I'll come talk to her class about body issues. Maybe it's because I'm a little drunk, but I write her back immediately to say yes. Then I close the computer and join the game. I'm really good at Mexicali.

My sociology class has gotten much easier since confrontation day. For one, I did get up the nerve to talk to Professor Kirby and tell him that I'm uncomfortable with the class discussing my personal involvement in an ad campaign. He was understanding, and he shifted the topic in the next class to a different ad with a similar feel. Also, I think I earned some of the other students' respect with the story I wrote for the paper. People are friendly to me now. Especially Oliver.

He catches me as I walk out of the sociology building and steps next to me as we head across the quad.

"Snack?" he asks.

"Sure," I say.

"My Retreat points are low," he says. "If we go there, you're buying."

I smile. We have this meal plan where you get a ton of points at the main dining hall, ACDC, but way fewer at the café-style Retreat.

"Split cheese fries with me and you're on," I say.

"Deal," says Oliver.

It's nice to sit with him for a while. We talk about Sociology, how much we miss having cable TV to watch twenty-four/seven, our hometowns. He's from somewhere in Connecticut, and he tells me about how fall is the greatest season there because of the color bursts from the leaves. We don't have to talk about fashion, or modeling, or anything besides what makes us *us*.

Eventually, I bring up the health class visit I'm planning on making tomorrow. I'm feeling so comfortable with Oliver that I kind of want his opinion.

"It sounds awesome," he says, scraping the last bit of melted American cheese off of the bottom of our shared plate.

"You think?" I ask. "It's not some hypocritical thing for me to do?"

"Why would it be?" he asks. "Because you're skinny? Does that mean you've never had body issues?"

"Hardly," I say.

"So go," he says. "People will listen to you because you seem to have this glamorous background, right? Why not use that power for good?"

"But with the ad I tried to—" I start.

"An ad is different," he says. "It's really impersonal and open to interpretation. To be honest, I thought that ad was a bit spurious."

"Oh," I say, looking down at the table and judging Oliver slightly for using a fancy word for *bogus*.

"But in person, Violet," says Oliver, lifting up my chin, "there's no way anyone could call you insincere."

My face tingles where Oliver touched it and I can feel my cheeks getting red. "Thanks," I say.

Then I hear Kurt's voice from the mailbox area across the way. "*Women's Wear*!" he shouts, running over to join me and Oliver.

"Do you really subscribe to a fashion trade magazine?" I ask. The only people I know who get *Women's Wear Daily* are modeling agents and magazine editors.

"Gregory has an internship at dailycandy.com," says Kurt, who has finally managed to hook up with his long-stalked object of affection. "He slipped this in the mail to me."

"He's a good boyfriend," I say, smiling.

"We haven't used that word yet!" says Kurt, hitting me on the arm with the rolled-up newsprint he's holding. "Don't jinx it!"

He unfolds *Women's Wear* and there's a copy of the Mirabella ad— this one starring Veronica. She's got the same "healthy body" message tag underneath her photo, which is a shot of her perched on the edge of what looks like a Lucite set of bleachers. She's in that knees-at-the-chest pose that kind of looks like she's squatting to pee, but is also a common fashion stance. Her arms are straight at her sides, resting on the bleacher too.

"Total rip-off of the *Nylon* Ashley Olsen cover from like two years ago," says Kurt.

"She looks gorgeous," I say.

"Well, duh!" says Kurt. "It's Veronica Trask."

Oliver grabs his bag and stands up to go. "See you later, Violet," he says. "I've got to go to work."

"Oh, where do you work?" I ask.

"The campus post office," he says, pointing toward the student mailboxes and smiling sheepishly.

"That's cool," I say, and I mean it. It's nice that he has a campus job.

I wave and watch him go. Then Kurt stops flipping through *Women's Wear* and looks up at me.

"Why so pouty?" he says. "Your ad looked good too!"

"It's not that," I say.

"Well if it's about your muffin top, I'd suggest laying off the cheese fries," says Kurt, sounding uncharacteristically catty. Well, it's uncharacteristic that it's targeted at me, at least.

I must look aghast because Kurt tries to backpedal. "Oh, I didn't mean you were fat," he says. "Just a little skinny-fat . . . like Gwyneth after a baby."

I stand up and push in my chair.

"It's nothing a little time with five-pound hand weights won't fix!" Kurt yells after me as I storm out of the Retreat. As if his screaming that across the room makes things better. Jeez.

I think all day about Kurt saying I have muffin top. I even turn sideways in my full-length mirror and pinch the skin at my hips. I guess I have put on a few pounds again, but now that I'm not under constant scrutiny from bookers and my agent, I just want to let go a little. When will being normal be okay?

ten

The next day as I get off the subway in Brooklyn, my heart is pounding. I asked Chloe if I could come in late to *Teen Fashionista*, and I told her what I was doing. I even thought maybe it could count as research or something for a body image story, so she told me to take notes while I'm visiting the high school.

I look around the block I'm on—there are three delis, two bars, a Chinese place, and a Thai place. This is near where Aunt Rita lives, I think. I haven't talked to her in a few weeks, but I know she'd be proud of what I'm doing today.

When I walk into the classroom, I feel thirty pairs of eyes on me. There are mostly girls and couple of guys in the class, and they seem young—like maybe freshmen. I realize I'm only a year out of high school, officially, but I feel way old standing in front of them.

"Class, this is Violet Greenfield," says the health teacher, Ms. Stone. "She's a student at Vassar College upstate, and she's also a fashion model."

I smile, feeling really awkward. "Hi," I say to no one in particular. Immediately, one girl raises her hand.

"Yes?" I call on her.

"Have you met anyone famous?" she asks.

"Um, not really," I say. "I mean, sometimes there are famous people at fashion shows or parties, but I've never talked to any of them."

"Why not?" a boy in the back of the room asks.

"I guess I'm shy," I say.

"I've read your blog on MySpace," says a girl to my left. "I'm xxangelxx and I always leave you comments."

"Thanks," I say. "I really love getting comments. Well, the nice ones anyway."

The class laughs, and I start to feel a little more at ease.

Ms. Stone holds up a copy of *Vogue*, the one with my Mirabella ad in it. "Violet is involved in a fashion campaign where she's suggesting that women should feel good about their bodies—whatever their size." She smiles at me and nods. "Why don't you tell us about that, Violet?"

"Well," I say, clearing my throat. "It started with the MySpace blog, actually, and I kept getting comments from girls . . . um, people . . . who were obsessed with being thin. I felt like there was something bad about that. And maybe something bad about what I was doing as a model. So I wanted to just tell people that it's okay to like yourself the way you are."

"But you're so skinny," says a girl in the front row with slicked-back hair and a diamond stud in her nose. "Why should we listen to you?"

I wasn't quite ready for that. My Sociology class has nothing on these kids. "I don't mean that I'm an authority," I say. "I just mean that I've had a lot of self-doubt like everyone."

"But you're a model," says a girl by the window with long braids. "It's different for you."

I glance up at the clock, and I realize I have to talk to this class for twenty-seven more minutes.

"Okay, your questions are fair, but let me tell you a little bit about Me in High School . . ."

When I arrive at *Teen Fashionista* that afternoon, I'm buzzing with excitement. I have pages and pages of notes on what the students said to me, the questions they asked, the issues they brought up.

"How'd it go?" asks Chloe, stopping by my cube and leaning on the open partition.

"Great!" I say. I sound more cheerful than I've ever sounded with her, but today I mind less that she's standing in the way of Me and Roger. "At first everyone was skeptical, but then we really got into what they thought about the Mirabella campaign and my involvement."

Chloe nods, seeming interested, so I keep going.

"They called me out on being skinny and preaching about body image at the same time," I say, "But then I was able to tell them about how insecure I felt just last year in high school, and how everyone nicknamed me 'the Jolly Green Giant' in eighth grade, and how one year at a middle school dance Kevin Murtaugh had to stand on the bleachers just to be able to slow-dance with me."

"No!" Chloe says, covering her mouth and laughing.

"Yes!" I scream, giggling along with her. "It was mortifying."

"Violet, you know what's a great story?" she asks.

"What?" I ask.

"You!" She points directly at me.

"Me? But you did that already—last year." *In fact, that's how you met my best friend and stole him away*, I think, remembering when Chloe came down to North Carolina to interview me.

"No, no," says Chloe, waving her hand dismissively. "That was like a profile of an up-and-coming model. We do those every month. I'm talking about the real you. The one those girls saw today."

"I don't get it," I say.

"Those details you just told me were really funny!" says Chloe. "They'd make any girl who looked up to you see what a genuine person you are."

I kind of hate it when Chloe says nice things to me. It makes it harder to despise her.

"Let me talk to Marilyn about it," she says. "If you're into it, that is."

"Sure," I say. "I've got nothing to hide."

And the more I think about it, the more I think doing that story might just be a great idea.

When I leave the office at six o'clock to catch the six-fifteen train back to Poughkeepsie, I feel a little sad. I haven't spoken to Roger since last week, except to IM about the fact that our favorite Lifetime movie, *Pretty Poison*, is rerunning soon. I'm not sure if he's mad or if he's just too busy with his own life to want to spend time with me anymore. And I'm not sure which one of those scenarios is worse.

As soon as I push through the glass doors at Bruton, I hear a familiar voice.

"Villainous Violet." My agent is leaning against the building's column smoking a cigarette.

"Angela?" I'm surprised to see her. "What are you doing here?"

"Just visiting another client," she says, her white veneers glowing despite the fact that she has a pack-a-day habit. Her dental bills must be astronomical.

"Oh," I say. I've been meaning to return her dozen calls and tell her that I don't want to work. At least not regularly and not while I'm in school. But I'm a chicken.

"We should talk," she says, in her typically direct manner. "I'm so glad I ran into you. Not that I could miss you these days." She looks me up and down.

"What does that mean?" I ask, folding my arms across my chest protectively.

"Nothing, darling," she says, pulling a hair from my coat shoulder. "You just seem to have bulked up a bit. But not to worry—we have a week before the shows so you have time to . . . adjust things."

"I'm healthy, Angela," I say. "I don't need to lose any weight."

"Well not if you're ready to do catalog work for a C-list department store," she says, holding her smile. "But you won't be walking any Fashion Week runways with those thighs."

The fact that she can't even see my thighs under my knee-length coat, but she still manages to insult them, annoys me.

"I have to go, Angela," I say.

"Fine, darling," she says. "I just wanted to say hello and tell you that people are asking about you for Fashion Week. Of course, there's talk that you're older now, maybe not the freshest face for the tents this season, and perhaps a bit of a loose cannon."

I stay silent. I won't let her bait me into asking for an insult.

"Still, people are mentioning you for castings," she continues. "You've always been good at keeping your name on everyone's lips, what with your blogging and your club escapades and visiting health classes at local high schools . . ."

"What?" I ask, almost choking on the cold air outside. "How did you know about that?"

"For such a young thing you're not as plugged into the blog world as I'd think," she says.

I raise my eyebrows. "Gawker?" I ask.

"Bingo," she says. "After all, you're still a model with a big campaign out, Venerated Violet. Don't think you're anonymous all of a sudden just because you're tucked away on a dreamy little campus upstate."

"My train leaves soon," I say, shifting my feet.

"Back to Vassar, dear?" she purrs. "Well, do enjoy yourself, but take a little tip from me: Beer has a hundred and fifty calories per bottle, but marijuana has zero."

I walk away from her, waving with my back turned as I head for Grand Central. *Angela's pushing drugs now?* I have a bad feeling she wasn't meeting someone at Bruton—she was staked out for me.

On the train home, I call Julie at Brown. I've tried her a few times in the past week, but I always get her voice mail. I don't blame her—I know she's busy and I haven't been leaving messages—but doesn't she realize that five missed calls from me means that I'm a little hard up?

"V!" she says into the phone, sounding out of breath.

"Jules? Is it really you?" I ask.

"Yes!" she says. "I'm late for a newspaper meeting so I'm running! But I had to answer." She pauses and then says, "Sorry I've been hard to get on the phone."

"Oh, it's okay," I say. I'm not into confrontation, even with Julie. "So why the Friday night meeting?"

"Oh, it's just because our editor is really intense and wants to dole out weekend assignments. Whatever! But anyway, how are you? How's Vassar?" she asks, sounding so upbeat and like she just *loves* college and her busy newspaper schedule. How can I tell her I'm feeling down about things?

"I'm good!" I say, willing myself to smile so I'll sound bright. "Things are really great!"

"Whoa," says Julie, her panting slowing. "What's wrong?"

"Oh, nothing," I say, realizing it's dumb to try to act fake with someone who's known me since I was five years old. "We can talk about it later."

"Oooh, I wish I had time right now," says Julie. "I just can't, V. I have to go to this meeting."

"It's okay," I say.

"Call me tomorrow, okay?" she says. I can tell she's already in her about-to-get-off-the-phone mode. "I have the afternoon totally free to study and procrastinate by talking to my best friend."

"Okay," I say, trying to sound cheery. We hang up and I toss my cell phone in my bag. I guess I can get some reading done.

When I get back to my room, Kurt is lying across my bed. "You were on Gawker!" he shouts.

"I know," I say, throwing down my bag with a thud. "I have a headache—don't make it any bigger."

"Ew," he says, sitting up and wrinkling his nose. "Press makes you cranky."

"Did they say I was fat?" I ask.

"Huh?" he says.

"Did Gawker say I was fat?!" I repeat.

"What? No!" says Kurt. "Of course not. Is this still about me calling you a Gwyneth? Because I take it back."

"It's not about that," I say, sinking down next to him on the bed.

"Tell Daddy what's the matter," Kurt says, stroking my hair.

"I'm just getting overwhelmed," I say. *How can I explain to someone I just met a few weeks ago that I'm having a major identity crisis?*

"I know what you need," says Kurt.

"What?" I ask, pouting doubtfully.

"A weekend away!" he shouts, jumping up and pulling a set of keys from his pocket. "I got the Saab!"

"Huh?" I ask.

"My older sister at Middlebury *always* has the car, but she dropped it off yesterday because she's sick of shoveling it out of the snow!" says Kurt. "It's parked in South Lot just waiting to take a road trip."

"Did somebody say *road trip*?!" Fan pops her head into my room with a grin. When Kurt's at full volume, there's no hiding anything.

"Somebody did," I say, cheering slightly. "And I think I know where we should go."

"Where?" ask Jess and Kurt at the same time.

"Brown."

eleven

The drive to Providence is pretty fun. Fan and Jess both sit in the backseat, while I get shotgun.

"Isn't it weird to just go away for the weekend and not even have to tell your parents?" says Jess.

Fan scoffs. "We're not twelve!" she says.

"I know what you mean," I say, looking back at Jess. Fan can be a little harsh sometimes.

"Yeah right, Miss World Traveler," says Kurt. "I'm sure you've flown to other *countries* without even checking in with your parents."

"Have not!" I say. But he's right—I did do that last year when Angela needed me to rush to Paris for Mirabella's show. Mom and Dad are busy with work and Jake's basketball and their own lives—and they don't really *get* me right now. They're still there for me and they love me, of course, but I feel like I'm moving into that friends-as-family zone. It's nice.

We plug in Kurt's iPod and listen to a mix of old Madonna and Kylie Minogue.

"I'm into Britpop," says Kurt, when I ask him about his playlist.

"Madonna's American," I say. "And isn't Kylie Australian?"

"First of all, Miss Madge is *hardly* American anymore," says Kurt authoritatively. "Secondly, Australia is just England for Party People—which is why I plan to go there for Junior Year Abroad!"

We laugh and sing and munch on gas station junk food all the way to Brown's gates.

Fan and Jess plan to go find one of Fan's friends from high school who's here—she's already agreed to have them crash on her floor. We promise to meet up tonight as they take their bags and pillows and start trekking across campus.

Then I call Julie. She screams and gives us directions to her room.

From the first second she opens her door, I know this is going to be the best weekend. Kurt gives Julie a giant hug, like he's known her for years, and she squeals with delight. Julie's roommate is gone for the weekend, so the bed situation is totally settled.

"You and me, Pretty V?" Kurt asks, jumping onto the room-mate's pink seersucker comforter.

"You wish," I say. "Good thing Julie and I are used to sharing a single bed—we did it at camp one summer when I was afraid to sleep by the dead flies caught in my window screen! Remember?"

"Duh, of course," says Julie. "And luckily you're still as skinny as you were when we were nine."

We spend the afternoon remembering stuff like that—how in first grade whenever I went to the bathroom and turned the Go sign to Stop to indicate I was in there, Roger would always maddeningly turn it back to Go; the way Julie and I used to pedal as fast as we could on our pink flower bikes to lose my little brother, Jake, who was always trailing us ("And then you went out with him!" I shout through a smile); the summer when Roger declared it "Dry Season" for no apparent reason and would *not* get wet (Julie and I conspired to push him into the pool just before summer ended).

"He was so pissed!" says Julie, leaning over in her chair and tearing up with laughter at the memory. "Remember his face when his precious glasses got soaked?!"

I can't speak, but I'm almost snorting from trying to control my giggles.

Even Kurt is cracking up.

"You guys had *normal* childhoods!" he laments, laughing. "I was too busy trying to figure out why my mother freaked out when I carried her gold clutch to the first day of third grade because it matched the metallic sneakers I'd picked out. I never got the Norman Rockwell Americana scenes!"

"Poor Kurt!" Julie and I say in unison.

Later, Julie takes us on a walking tour of campus and we spend a while sitting at the Blue Room, an on-campus café where she buys us snacks with her meal plan points. We hear all about the newspaper and its incestuous dating scene. Julie has a crush on a junior—her editor.

"Switching to older guys?" I ask her.

"I think so," she says, eyes shining. "It's good to try new things, right?"

"Yup," I say, smiling back at her. It's kind of a relief that she's over my brother. It wasn't like I hated that they were dating last year, but it did make things a little awkward sometimes.

"And older guys who are like your boss, too," says Kurt. "You are such a power whore!"

"I am," she says, nodding as she sips her Diet Coke. "Totally."

I smile. I love how they're getting along.

That night we meet up with Fan and Jess—plus Fan's friend Ruth and her roommate—to hit a party in a dorm called Perkins. I'm working through a crowd toward the keg with Kurt at my back. He's holding onto the belt loop of my jeans so he doesn't get lost in the mash of people, and he's yelling, "Supermodel on the line! Raise the velvet ropes!"

I'd be embarrassed, but no one is even listening to him—the music is loud and I'm feeling fairly incognito on this visit. Not one person has said anything to me about being a model. It's kind of nice.

We finally get our cups filled and head over to where Julie is talking to some newspaper friends, when I stop suddenly. Kurt runs into my back, spilling half of his new, hard-won beer down my white silk tank top.

"Bitch, what?" he says, staring up to follow my gaze.

"It's Oliver," I whisper, half to myself to make sure I'm seeing right.

"What is that boy doing here?" muses Kurt. "Well, whatever. It just means we know more people at Brown than we thought we did. We're popular!"

He grabs my free hand and pulls me toward Julie's crowd, where Oliver is just being introduced around the circle.

Julie turns to us. "Oh, and these are *my* friends who are visiting from Vassar—Violet and Kurt," she says.

"Hey," says Oliver, smiling at me.

"Oooh," says Julie, exaggerating her response like kids do in elementary school when someone's in trouble. "So you guys already know each other."

How could she tell?

"We do," says Oliver. "I work on the newspaper at Vassar, and Violet wrote a great piece for us."

"We're also both in Intro Soc," I add, feeling flushed.

"And Oliver and I used to sleep together but I dumped his ass for a sophomore hottie!" says Kurt, raising his cup.

Everyone stares at him, including me.

"*Joking!*" he shouts, and we all break a smile. "Jeez, you Brown people are really uptight."

It's crazy that Oliver is here, but also exciting. It's nice to hang out with him this way. We end up talking until four a.m., when the party winds down and Julie's asleep with her head in my lap.

"We should go," I say. "I think your friends left like an hour ago."

"Yeah," says Oliver. "And I think that girl wants her bed back." I look over and see the party's hostess sleeping upright in her desk chair.

"Oops!" I whisper, laughing as I gently wake Julie and we all start to tiptoe out of the room. When we get outside, Oliver's going right and we're going left. Julie walks slightly ahead of us.

"Good night, Violet," says Oliver, taking my hand and pressing it to his lips. "Sweet farewell."

"Good night," I say, laughing a little and wondering if he's being cheesy because he's drunk. I look up at him. It's nice to look up at someone—he must be six feet four. His hand lingers on mine for a moment before he breaks our hold and turns to go. I spin around and jog a few steps to catch up with Julie.

"He *liiikes* you," she giggles drunkenly.

"Shh!" I say. "He'll hear you!" But I smile as I link my arm through hers. I think she might be right.

After the weekend at Brown and a week back on campus at Vassar, I'm dreading my Friday in the city at *Teen Fashionista*. I just start to feel normal, like I don't have anything to live up to except being a regular old college freshman, and then I'm walking back through the doors of Bruton and where everyone stares at me. The elevator is the worst—I can feel other girls looking me up and down and judging my shoes.

Angela left me three messages this week, all of them with an urgent tone. She wants me to do a go-see for Fashion Week, which is starting, like, right now.

"There haven't been many calls since the photo of you visiting that school went up online," she says. I'm returning her message from my cube at *Teen Fashionista*. "Actually, just one."

"Really?" I ask, wondering if she's going to tell me to start going to more parties or being seen around town like Veronica has been this month—I can't open the *Post* without seeing her on Page Six.

"The proof is in the picture, Voluminous Violet," she says bluntly. "And New York Fashion Week just isn't kind to fat girls."

My eyes well up a little, but I blink really fast to get rid of the tears. I should be more angry than sad—*hello!* I'm a healthy weight and I'm still thin by normal standards—but her comment stings. "I guess this isn't the Fashion Week for me then," I say, hoping this means I can get out of the go-see and avoid the humiliation.

"We'll see about that," says Angela. "I've been honest about your un-runway proportions, and someone wants to see you anyway. You'll stop by Tracetown tonight before you run back to campus—Mickey and Matt will be waiting at seven p.m."

I consider blowing off the appointment, but I'm glad I don't because when I get to Tracetown's Soho offices, Mickey races to the door to hug me. Theirs was the first runway I ever walked, and Mickey has always been effusively complimentary toward me. Matt gives the vibe that he likes me too, but he doesn't say much.

"My beauty!" says Mickey as he opens his arms and pulls back to look at me. I'm glad for my bulky winter coat as his eyes run up my body. It's a designer-on-model stare that I'm just not comfortable with right now.

"I know I've gained some weight," I say quietly.

Matt snorts in the corner and Mickey shoots him an angry look. But when he turns back to me, his eyes are kind.

"Not to worry, Violet," he says. "We have something special in mind for you." He pulls out a red jewel-tone, floor-length goddess dress in hammered satin.

"It's beautiful," I say. And it is. It looks like something you'd wear to the Met Costume gala—more like couture than the ready-to-wear stuff that Tracetown normally does.

"We don't care that you're not a size zero at the moment," says Mickey, hanging the dress back up carefully on its perch by the window of their loft. "Ours was your first runway, and we want you to walk with us again—you'll close the show in this gown."

"I'd love to," I say. And I really mean it.

"I also want to introduce you to Basil Malicsi, our new apprentice," says Mickey, pointing toward the clothing racks. "He's a huge fan of yours."

I peer through the fog from the steamer and see a gorgeous, dark-haired guy who looks about my age. He's de-wrinkling the gowns, but he stops working and smiles when I say hello. His perfectly shaggy-shaped bangs hang over wide brown eyes, and he wears a fantastic beaded necklace over his black turtleneck.

"Basil grew up in the Philippines," says Matt, breaking his usual code of silence. "He's one to watch."

Basil must be a good designer, I think. And then I remember—

Fan! I know she'd love it if I brought up the green cosmetics campaign.

"My roommate is Filipina," I say. "Actually, she's really into environmentalism . . ."

Matt rolls his eyes, but Mickey listens to me talk about how passionate people are getting about getting the harsh chemicals out of their products.

"I love it," he says, when I finish. "Environmentalism is very chic."

I smile. Fan would be launching into a rant about how it's not "chic," it's a long-term commitment that is very serious, but I'm just happy Mickey didn't blow me off.

"Tell you what, Violet," he says. "I'll get in touch with some of the earth-friendly companies and ask them about doing makeup for the show."

"Thanks, Mickey," I say, glad that I spoke up.

When I walk out of Tracetown and onto the cold streets of Soho, I feel exhilarated. I want to call Angela and tell her that I'm bookable even at a normal-girl size. I'm bookable because I'm *me*.

My phone rings, but it's not a number I know.

"Hello?" I answer tentatively.

"Violet?" says a guy's voice.

"Yeah," I say.

"It's Oliver," he says.

"Oh, hi," I say, smiling to myself.

"I was wondering if maybe you and your friends wanted to come to this party my hall's throwing in Raymond tonight," he says. "We got a keg and it should be pretty packed."

"That sounds fun," I say. "I'm in the city but I'm about to get the train back. I should be there in a couple of hours."

"Great," Oliver says. "We'll probably start around eleven or so."

"Okay," I say. "See you later."

"Later," he says.

When I hang up I decide that I'll get a cab up to Grand Central so I can catch the eight twenty-nine p.m. train and get up to Vassar early. This party requires some getting ready.

Just as I shut the taxi door and direct the driver to Forty-second and Lexington, my phone rings again.

"If I could do it all again . . . I'd go back and change everything" blares from my phone.

"Hey, Roger," I say.

"Where are you?" he asks.

"Downtown," I say. "I'm going to Grand Central to get the train back to Poughkeepsie."

"What if I asked you to come over instead?" he says.

I pause for just a moment before I tell the driver to turn around.

"I'll be there in five minutes," I say.

twelve

When I get over to Roger's dorm, he's pacing the lobby downstairs.

"What's wrong?" I ask as I pull off my winter hat and shake my snow-covered boots.

"I'm freaking out," he says. "I have an art history exam Monday and for some reason I can't keep the paintings in my head. I really need your help."

"Wouldn't it be better to study with someone in your class?" I ask, annoyed that he dragged me out here to *study*. For some reason I thought—maybe hoped—that he was going to tell me he and Chloe broke up. Is that wrong?

"I know you can help me, V," he says. "Remember junior year when I had so much trouble with the Latin vocab review? You weren't even *taking* Latin, but you still found ways to make me remember every single word. I aced that test!"

I smile at the memory. I made up rhymes, visual cues, and even songs to help Roger keep those words in his head. I raise my eyebrows at him.

"Please?" he says, getting down on one knee and taking my still-gloved hand. "Go back to Vassar tomorrow. I really need your help tonight."

And what can I do? "Okay," I say.

Roger kisses my hand, stands up, and presses the elevator button.

"My roommate's out of town," he says. "You can crash on his bed."

I'm feeling slightly guilty about bailing on Oliver and my friends, but I push it out of my mind. One thing that helps: upstairs, Roger has a snack station set up with my favorites—Chex Mix, mini York Peppermint Patties, and a six-pack of Coke.

"Coke!" I scream. My year of modeling got me off nondiet soda, but it is amazing when I let myself indulge.

"Not just Coke," says Roger, pulling a can out of his mini-fridge. "Sweaty Coke!"

He knows I love it when condensation runs down the can. Julie used to claim that was purely an aesthetic thing, but Roger and I agree that sweaty Cokes taste the best.

"Open one now," I say.

"I'll open two," he says. "Now grab those flash cards and quiz me."

We spend about six hours running through flash cards and looking up art online—and I think of tricks for Roger to memorize things. Like, Byzantine art is abstract and symbolic, so I told him to remember that "The *Byzantines* are *busy* so they don't have time to get all deep and realistic with their art." Around two a.m., we take a break and lie back onto our respective beds.

"Are these even standard twin size?" asks Roger, pondering the skinniness of his dorm mattress while I silence a third call on my cell from Kurt.

"I think there's a special college-size bed that's just really narrow," I say. "But they're longer, too, which I appreciate."

"That's perfect for you, Miss Runway," Roger says, propping himself up on one elbow to face me. "As long as you're sleeping alone."

I stare up at the ceiling and will myself not to face Roger. *Does he care whether I'm sleeping alone?* I'm not sure I want to give away the fact that I am currently stone-cold single.

"Yeah," I say quietly. We're silent for a few beats.

And then Roger says, "Remember those beds in Barcelona?"

"Totally." I laugh, turning to face his bed.

"That room was ridiculous!" he says. Last year when Roger visited me in Spain, we stayed in a hostel where the beds were so close together they were practically a double. And I remember that we slept back to back after that too-much-sangria evening where he kissed me for the first—and only—time.

I start to feel self-conscious recalling that night, so I lie back down on the bed and refocus my eyes on a crack in the ceiling. Roger sighs and I hear him lie back too. *Was that sigh nostalgic? Like maybe he thinks about our kiss sometimes too?* I decide to take a chance.

"Do you ever think about that night?" I ask softly.

"Huh?" asks Roger. "What did you say?"

"Um, do you ever think about that night in Barcelona?" I repeat.

"Sometimes," Roger says. His answer is too cryptic for me to interpret whether he thinks about it positively, or with regret, or with anger, and I'm too much of a chicken to press him further, so I stay quiet.

"It was good that we didn't follow my harebrained scheme to

travel around Europe together," Roger continues, smiling and sitting up with a renewed energy. "What a dumb idea!"

"Yeah," I say. My voice sounds faint. I can't admit to Roger that I often wonder wistfully about what it would have been like if I'd taken him up on his offer to travel with me—maybe we would have started the romance that always should have been. But Angela called to offer me a runway in Paris, and I jumped on a plane. I left. And now I have to look around Roger's dorm room and see eleven photos of Chloe.

"Back to the flash cards?" Roger asks.

"One more run-through," I agree, sitting up and willing myself to snap out of my reverie. "Then dessert."

"The Peppermint Patties?" asks Roger.

"Of course!" I say. So far I've limited myself to the snack mix.

"Let's get one now," he says. He reaches into the mini-fridge, where he's keeping them because he knows I like the patties cold. Maybe it was all the commercials they used to have with snow and ice, but it just seems like a cold-eating candy.

I stand next to the fridge and lean into Roger as he pulls off the wrapper and tosses it aside. He puts the patty next to my ear and then snaps it in half. *Psssssst.*

"Amazing," I say. When Roger and I were younger, we heard that Peppermint Patties make a hissing noise when you break them close to your ear. Unlike the stories about Pop Rocks and Coke breaking someone's jaw, and the one about how a tooth left in a glass of soda will dissolve overnight (both of which we also tried for ourselves), the patty factoid is not an urban legend—it's totally true.

I take my half and break it into quarters next to Roger's ear. *Psssssst.*

"Isn't this just the most wonderful thing in the world?" he asks, turning to me with his eyes lit up like we're six years old and just discovering this trick.

"Yes," I say. "It really is."

When I get back to Vassar the next day, Fan is lying on the couch in our suite living room, reading.

"Missed you last night," she says without looking up from her book.

"Oh, yeah," I say. "I, um, had to stay in the city."

"What for?" she asks, raising her eyes from the page.

"I had this modeling thing," I say.

"Oh," she says. "And then you stayed at your aunt's?"

"Yeah," I say, grateful for her presumption. I'm not sure why I don't want to tell her I stayed with Roger.

"Cool," she says, turning back to her book.

When I head into my room, I hear a familiar voice outside my interior window.

"Violet! Is that you?" Kurt's knocking on the mottled glass, so I open the window onto the hallway. He leans on the sill with both elbows, which makes his butt stick way out.

I know I owe him an explanation for not picking up his calls yesterday—I put my phone on vibrate after the first few, so Roger and I wouldn't be interrupted.

"Someone missed you last night," he says teasingly.

"I know," I say. "Kurt, I'm sorry I didn't tell you I wasn't coming back."

He dismisses me with a wave of his hand. "It wasn't me who missed you, honey," he says. "It was Oliver."

"Really?" I ask, feeling a flutter of excitement. "What did he say?"

"He just kept asking if I'd heard from you, telling me to call you, and basically being a pathetic lovesick hetero." Kurt rolls his eyes. "But I knew you had something going in the city. Dish."

"It was just a modeling appointment," I say.

"Uh-uh," says Kurt, wagging his finger from side to side. "Oliver told me he talked to you *post*-appointment and that you told him you were on your way back. So what interrupted? A hot stranger on the six-train? Veronica Trask and an unbelievable VIP pass to Marquee?"

"No, nothing like that," I say. "I just got a call from Roger—you know, my friend from high school?"

"Yeah, yeah," he says.

"He has a big art history test on Monday, and he really needed my help studying," I say.

"Uh-huh," says Kurt, nodding his head. I can tell he wants me to hurry up and get to the exciting part.

"That's it," I say.

"That's what?" Kurt says, looking confused.

"That's all," I say. "That's why I stayed in the city last night."

"Wait—hold on," says Kurt. He opens the window wider and swings one leg into my room, then the other, until he ends up sitting cross-legged on my bed next to me. He slams the window shut. "You're telling me that you stayed in the city—passing up a party that Oliver, whom you totally have a crush on, personally invited you to—to help your friend from high school *study*?"

"Yeah," I say, shrugging my shoulders like it's no big deal. When Kurt spells it out like that, though, it does seem fishy.

"Hmph," he says. "So how long have you been in love with this Roger guy?"

"I'm not," I say. *Do not get red. Do not get red.* But I can already feel the blood rushing to my cheeks.

"Let's dispense with the denials," says Kurt. "It's okay to have a boyfriend from home who you don't really want people on campus to know about. It's smart, really. You get to play both locations."

He smiles at me devilishly, like he's in on some super-devious secret I've been keeping.

"Roger's not my boyfriend," I say. "I swear."

"So then why are you glowing like you just spent the night with either the greatest one-night stand in history or the love of your life?" asks Kurt.

"He's my best friend in the world," I say.

"Oh man," says Kurt. "We're in deeper than I thought."

thirteen

When I see Oliver in Sociology on Monday, I smirk sheepishly. He grins back with a full, megawatt smile, making me feel even more guilty for ditching him.

"Hey," I say.

"Hey," he says.

"Um, sorry I missed Friday night," I say. "I heard it was really fun." *I'm such a dork.*

"Oh, yeah," he says. "No big deal. I mean, I wish you could've come, but I guess you had—"

"It was this modeling appointment in the city," I lie. "After I talked to you they wanted me to go back for another fitting and it just got really late, so I stayed over at my aunt's house."

I'm amazed at how easily the deception rolls off my tongue.

"And she has this thing where she hates cell phones so she made me turn mine off and I couldn't get in touch with anyone," I continue. When did I get so good at lying?

"That's cool," says Oliver. "So you're modeling again?"

"Just a runway show," I say, glad that I don't have to defend a print ad or something more "insidious."

"Oh," he says. And he says it in such a way that I feel like he has more to say.

"What does that mean?" I ask.

"Um, nothing really," he says.

"Seriously—what?" I ask.

"I just wish you were around more on the weekends," he says, smiling. "It would be fun to hang out like we did at Brown."

"It would be," I say. Is it wrong to love Roger and really, really *like* Oliver?

Of course, the week that Oliver turns on the flirt is the busiest week of my year. I have to get fitted for the gown at Trace-town on Wednesday, and I'm set to walk their runway at one p.m. on Friday, which means I'll miss a half day at *Teen Fashionista*. Luckily, most of the editors will be at the shows anyway, so the office will be dead. Or so Chloe tells me when I request the afternoon off.

It's been several months since I walked a runway—the last one was for Mirabella Prince in Paris when I freaking *fainted* in front of a huge crowd of fashion's Double A-List. Yikes.

But with Mickey and Matt, I feel at ease. They've made the gown fit perfectly around me, and even though I'm not a beanpole right now, I almost want to start singing that Natalie Wood song from *West Side Story* because, well, I feel pretty!

"Violet, I'm impressed that you had us go green for this show," says Henry, my favorite makeup artist who always works with Tracetown. "I don't usually like to switch up my makeup bag, but I'm into it!"

I look around and realize that—true to his word—Mickey has gotten donations from some of the most environmentally friendly companies out there. I smile.

"And don't worry about those nasty girls," Henry continues. "You just do your thing."

"What girls?" I ask. I look around and see stony model faces staring at me. One über-blond girl has her lip curled as she looks me up and down, a Tyra clone in the corner is staring at me with narrowed eyes, and the girl who just left the makeup chair turns to look over her shoulder at me and mouth *Whatever*.

I suddenly feel incredibly insecure.

"What's the deal?" I whisper to Henry through clenched teeth.

"Oh, they're just mad that you're closing the show, mad that your gown was altered to be bigger, mad that they're just not as naturally flawless as Miss Violet—you name it!"

"Really?" I ask, shocked that (a) anyone cares about me anymore—it's not like I'm particularly competitive this Fashion Week, and (b) I didn't notice their cold-shoulder treatment earlier. Now that Henry's pointed it out to me, I'm feeling less pretty by the second.

By the time the show starts, I'm having to consciously will my shoulders not to bunch up in the classic defensive posture I wore all through high school when I felt too tall, geeky, and generally FUG.

"What's the matter, Violet?" whispers Mickey when he takes my arm to walk out and close the show.

"Nothing," I lie, forcing the huge smile that I know he wants the cameras on the runway to see. We walk out into a sea of flashbulbs and I give them what they want—the smile that made me famous last year at my very first show for Tracetown, the one that got fashionista.com buzzing about the fresh-faced girl from North Carolina and traveled through the grapevine to *Women's Wear Daily* and magazines that later wanted to book me for shoots. It's the same smile that launched my career. But this time, it's fake.

After the show, I change into my street clothes and plan on heading straight back to the office. When I duck out of the tents—sunglasses on even though it's overcast and my big bulky coat serving as a buffer from the rest of the world—I hear a familiar voice.

"Violet!"

It's Veronica. She's probably walking twenty shows this week. I'm not sure I can face her.

"Hey," I say, opening my arms slowly for a hug.

"That was great!" she says.

"What? The show?" I ask. *She was watching?*

"Well, I had a break in the schedule and I knew you were closing Tracetown, so the PR girls let me slip in," she says. "You were wonderful."

"Are you being sarcastic?" I ask.

"No!" she says, looking hurt that I'd even ask. "V—I mean it."

"I'm not exactly model-sized anymore," I say. "They had to let the dress out for me."

"But that's what was so cool," says Veronica. "Not to mention the green cosmetics thing, which everyone is buzzing about in the tents. I'm sure there'll be lots of backtalk about you—blogs and whatever—but at the end of the day, isn't this what you wanted? To be yourself and be a role model?"

"Yeah, it is," I say tentatively.

"I have to run," says Veronica, grabbing onto my hand. "But promise me one thing?"

"What?" I ask.

"That you'll be proud of what you did today," she says, sounding more sincere than I've ever heard her. "I've never seen you look more beautiful."

She squeezes my hand and rushes off to her next show. I take a deep breath and resolve to walk with my head high. Maybe Veronica's right. Maybe I did just do a good thing.

When I get back to the *Teen Fashionista* office to finish up the day, I can feel a weird vibe. The second I sit down in my cube, I get an IM from Chloe ("Chlover" on IM—but when Julie and I are being catty, we agree it should be "Cougar" because she's so too old for Roger) telling me that Angela has called four times in the last hour. She started stalking Chloe when she couldn't get through to me.

VIOLET GREENFIELD: how did she sound?
CHLOVER: mad
VIOLET GREENFIELD: like mad that she couldn't reach me or
       mad in a bigger sense?
CHLOVER: bigger

My heart sinks.

VIOLET GREENFIELD: ok
VIOLET GREENFIELD: thanks

I pick up the phone and decide to just do it. I call Angela. Before the first ring is even halfway over, she's yelling.

"Venal Violet—how could you do this to me?"

"Do what?" I ask, honestly unsure.

"I told you last week that you needed to *do something* about your figure, and you blatantly ignored me!" she shouts. I cringe at the thought that everyone at the Tryst offices is hearing this tirade. "You walked a runway as a plus-size girl!! And Matt and Mickey *let you*? I should never work with them again! I should bar them from using Tryst girls! I should—"

"I am not plus-size," I interrupt, speaking quietly but assertively. I'm getting tired of Angela's abuse. Something in my tone stops her diatribe. "And even if I were, what would that matter as long as someone wants to book me? You're still getting your fee, Angela."

She stays quiet—which is a first—and I take that as a cue to keep going.

"I feel better than I ever have," I say. "I'm not starving myself or overeating, I'm not obsessing about who's booking me and who's not, I'm not Googling my own name every two seconds to find out what bad press is being written. I'm just having fun at school and making new friends and being myself."

Angela lets out a little snort of disgust.

"Reading self-help books these days, are we, Vile Violet?" she asks evilly. "Well, darling, you're just lucky Mirabella is so taken with Veronica that she hasn't minded me keeping you in the closet, so to speak."

"What do you mean?" I ask.

"Well, of course Mirabella's been wanting you to do all the appearances and press conferences and interviews that go along with being a part of this big campaign," says Angela. "But I've been telling her you're sick or unavailable—I couldn't let her see you with all that pudge in your cheeks." My hand instinctively reaches up to my face.

Then Angela delivers her big blow: "Our Veronica is always willing to take the spotlight, as you know."

My heart starts beating a little faster. *Was Veronica messing with me today? Is she really glad that I'm no longer in the top-model category? Does she want me out of the way?* The silence between me and Angela grows louder. I know she knows I'd be hurt if Veronica were betraying me in any way. I also know that Angela is capable of major manipulation to get what she wants. And what she wants is for me to lose weight, get back into modeling, and make her more freaking money.

I think back to the tents, and I remember the sincerity in Veronica's eyes as she told me she was proud of me—and how she's been there for me consistently since I helped her get into rehab last summer.

"Veronica's my friend," I say to Angela. "If she's doing the press for Mirabella Prince, that's fine with me."

There's a brief pause, but then Angela recovers. "Fabulous, darling," she says. I'm sure she's annoyed that her manipulation didn't work, but she's hiding it well. "I just have one more request."

"What?" I ask, expecting her to ask me to drop out of college or get on a flight to India or something equally ludicrous. The crazy thing is that in the past, I would have done it. I have always done what Angela asks.

"Don't cause a scene or talk to the press, please," she says.

"About what?" I ask.

"I'm dropping you." She just says it, like she's saying, "I'm canceling dinner" or "I have a cold."

"Huh?" I say.

"You're gone, Violet," she says. "You're no longer a Tryst girl."

I stare at my computer screen blankly and shake my head. It's like I can't even comprehend what she's is saying. Then I pull my thoughts together.

"Is this because of today?" I ask. "Because you didn't like the way I looked in *one runway show*?"

"It's not up for discussion, Vacating Violet," says Angela. "It's over."

And then there's a dial tone.

After a few moments of shock, I resolve to try to get some work done. I have a list of research projects that Chloe wants me to do—finding subjects for our "One Girl's Story" section, scouring newspapers for new health studies, Googling "mother-daughter competition." But I can't concentrate.

I grab my coat and walk to the elevator bank. I pass a few editors who say things like, "Good job today!" and "You're back at work after walking a show? That's commitment!" I smile. It's nice to be noticed. Is that part of my life over now that Angela dropped me?

I head downstairs and push through the glass doors into the frigid winter air. If I smoked, I'd light up right here outside the building. A lot of people do that, and it does look like it could relieve stress, but it's just so smelly. Instead, I breathe in the cold air as I lean against the gray stone wall. I close my eyes and sigh.

"Violet?"

I'm so upset that I'm hallucinating.

"Violet?"

I open my eyes. He's really there.

"Roger," I say. And then I collapse onto his shoulder, getting his coat wet with the tears I've been holding in.

"Whoa," he says, patting my back with his gloved hands and pulling me in tighter. "It's okay. Whatever it is, it's okay."

We stand like that for a minute or two—me crying, him rubbing my back. I silently acknowledge how amazing it is that Roger just showed up—like magic—when I needed him.

When I pull away, I apologize. "I got you wet," I say, sniffling. "And that's a new coat, too, isn't it?"

"Eh," he says, "It's H&M."

We laugh together for a moment. And then I tell him about the show, and Angela dropping me. I'm afraid he'll judge me. I'm afraid he'll say, "Good riddance to modeling!" I'm afraid he'll discount my mixed emotions. But he doesn't.

"Violet, I'm sorry," he says, pulling me in for another hug. "This is a hard day, huh?"

"Yeah," I say, glad that he's not doing the usual guy thing of proposing a thousand ways to fix what's wrong when all a girl really wants is some sympathy and maybe a little time to talk it out.

"Do you think we could hang out tonight?" I ask, knowing that he'll recognize the urgency of today, knowing that he'll make everything okay with a movie and a sweaty Coke. Knowing that he'll be there for me.

"Oooh," he says, looking down at his watch—a new one, I realize. A Cartier. *Since when do college freshmen wear Cartiers?* "Tonight's no good. I'm actually here to pick up Chloe a little early—we're going away for the weekend, up to her mom's house in the Catskills."

What?

I must look dumbfounded because, after an awkward pause, Roger continues. "It's a great place, really," he says.

My jaw drops open a little. *He's been to Chloe's mother's house?*

"I mean, I've seen pictures of it and it seems great," he says, backpedaling at my shocked stare. "This is our first trip together." He smiles as if I'm supposed to be happy for him. He smiles as if *he's* happy with Chloe.

"Oh," I say, wiping at a stray tear that's left over from my break-down. "That's nice."

"You don't really need me to stay here, do you?" asks Roger. "I mean, you've got your friends at Vassar to talk to and you'll be okay, right?"

"Totally," I say, trying to be nonchalant. Trying to pretend like he didn't just crush my heart and sabotage my idea of fate.

"Good," he says. "I wouldn't want you to be mad at me."

I force a smile.

"Should we go up to the office?" he asks.

And then I ride up in the Bruton elevators with my best friend/true love, while he's on the way to pick up his girlfriend.

How did this happen exactly?

fourteen

When I get back to campus, I'm glad to find that no one is around in my suite. I flop down on the bed and drop my iPod into its speaker set. It's on random but the first song that plays is Fergie's "Big Girls Don't Cry." Maybe it *is* time that I move on from the past. If Roger's with Chloe, then that's that. I stand up and stare at the standard-issue dorm hanging mirror, but I'm not looking at myself. I'm looking at a yellow piece of paper—the poem from Barcelona. I translate it in my head for the six hundredth time: "No more than friends, no less than true love." Yeah, right.

I reach up and gently pull the tape off the glass. Then I lean over to my bookshelf and grab *Lonely Planet*. I press the poem into the front of my guidebook to Spain. It's a memory.

I turn on my computer, and even though I know I shouldn't, I head straight for the blogs. When I type my name into technorati, I'm hit with an overload of information. It seems that everyone has an opinion about whether I should be walking the runway this season. Some people are snarky, some tepid, some downright evil ("Violet Greenfield made Tracetown's closing red gown look like a Spanish matador's oversized bull's-eye blanket"). Whatever that means. I feel tears creeping up, but I'm so sick of crying that I push them down. I close all the browser windows at once and vow to stay offline until some other model attracts the mean bloggers' ire.

There's a knock on the suite door. It can't be Kurt—he'd never knock. I glance in the mirror to make sure my eyes aren't red, pinch my cheeks to give them a little color, and walk over to open the door.

"Oliver, hi," I say. He's standing there with a bunch of daisies.

"Here," he says, handing the flowers to me. "For your big runway show."

I smile and step back so he can come into the common area. He sits down on our semiclean brown futon.

"So how'd it go today?" he asks, seeming genuinely interested.

"You haven't looked on style.com yet?" I ask, fingering the white flower petals.

"Um, no," he says earnestly. "Did you want me to? Because I'm happy to look it up and—"

"It went okay," I interrupt. But then I sigh a little.

"Just okay?" he asks.

"Well, I'm a little, um, bigger than the other girls," I say, setting the bouquet down on the coffee table and tucking my feet underneath me as I sit next to Oliver. "And they let me know it."

"Who did?" asks Oliver, his back straightening indignantly.

"The other models, bloggers, my agent," I say. And then I decide to tell Oliver about Angela. Why not? "Actually, my agent dropped me today."

"Oh," says Oliver, looking pensive. "That's bad, right? You wanted to keep modeling and be in school too?"

"I don't know," I say, thinking about Oliver's question. "I guess I don't really want to do both."

"So you're glad to be off the hook?" he asks cheerfully, looking hopeful.

"Not really," I say.

He looks at me quizzically. I wonder if he's thinking I don't want to lose the money, or I'm some vain girl who needs the attention. I don't want him to assume that, but I'm not sure I want to open up to him.

"I really like you, you know?" he says, looking right into my eyes.

"I like you too," I say.

"It's not because you're a model," he says. "It's because I think you're really smart, and thoughtful, and kind."

"Thanks," I say, wondering whether Oliver really knows me at all. I also think about how before I was a model no guys like Oliver—tall, blond, dimpled—ever looked in my direction. He's handsome and charming, and I was invisible, a high school nerd, the incredible shrinking Violet.

"So you're okay?" Oliver asks.

"I don't know," I say honestly.

"Well, would you smile if I asked you to be my date for tonight's all-campus party?" he asks.

I smile. "Yes," I say, internally resolving to let go of modeling, the city, Roger, and all the things that cause me pain. Because right now, college life is feeling like a good thing.

Oliver has to run back to his room to do some reading before we go out tonight, but he promises to come by around nine to pregame with me, Kurt, Fan, and Jess. When Fan walks into the room, I'm stretched out on the couch with Kate Chopin's *The Awakening*, feeling relaxed and content.

"No drama today?" she asks, opening the mini-fridge for a can of Dr Pepper.

"Well, some other models leered at my weight gain, my agent dropped me, and my best friend chose his new girlfriend over me, but other than that all's okay," I say, smiling.

"Whoa," says Fan. "Why so calm then?" She pushes my feet out of the way and sits down on the couch with me.

"I'm letting it go," I say, putting down my book and sounding almost convinced.

"I'm proud of you," Fan says, slapping my calf affectionately.

"You are?" I ask.

"Yes!" She smiles. "You got Tracetown to go green. You're a trailblazer, Violet. You don't realize the influence you have, and you're using it for *Good*."

"I didn't think about it being a big deal," I say.

"But it is," she says. "Thank you."

Who knew I was turning into Violet Greenfield, Environmental Activist?

"*Vi-o-let-a!*" shouts Kurt from the hall. I can hear him running down the hall to get to the door. Fan rolls her eyes at me and smiles. I laugh.

"Yes, Kurt?" I ask, as his tall, skinny frame appears in the doorway.

"I just left you a comment! You were so hot today at Tracetown!" he gushes.

"Aw, thanks," I say.

"Not everyone thought so," says Fan, not unkindly.

"What do you mean?" asks Kurt, shooting Fan a harsh lip-curl look. "Everyone who's posting on Violet's MySpace profile is a fan."

"Really?" I ask, standing up to grab my laptop. I bring it back into the common room and log on to myspace.com/violetgreenfield. I scroll through the comments:

lovewillcometoyou94: you look prettier than ever!!! and your makeup was soooo kewl that it was all green!!

Carolinababy919: girls from carolina look always good but u top them all :-) btw: i was born in chapel hill!!

Ann[M]isinlike: i want to let u know that u are a great model for girls who are real ppl, and u are very beautiful strong woman!!!!!!

There are dozens—and 99 percent of them are totally positive. There's even a post from Basil, Tracetown's apprentice, thanking me for walking "so ethereally, like old royalty." I look up at Kurt.

"My agent dropped me today," I say. But I'm smiling.

"That bitch!" he says. Then he squeezes in between me and Fan on the couch.

"Eff her!" adds Fan. "It's the people who matter—not The Man."

"You think?" I ask.

"Her loss, gorgeous," says Kurt. "You are a fan favorite."

I kiss his cheek. "Thanks for showing me this," I say.

That night, Oliver joins me, Kurt, Fan, and Jess in our pregaming. We have a ton of beer and a few delicious snacks— Funyuns, cheese puffs, Oreos—the perfect Friday dinner.

They all know about my fight with Angela and how I'm no longer with Tryst. And no one seems to care one bit. When I pull on an easy, soft knit dress to go to the party, I pair it with flip-flops. After all, a girl's gotta be able to dance—especially if no one is judging her toes.

This week has been the best ever, and it's made me realize that I really do want to create this college life—I don't need the city or the modeling industry, or even my magazine internship for that matter. I did have to change my cell phone number, though. Reporters kept calling and I'm not in the mood to talk—as much as Kurt wants to answer and bad-mouth Angela.

I almost decided to just not go back to *Teen Fashionista*, but Kurt convinced me that I shouldn't quit. "It's just Fridays until the end of the semester!" he said. "It's a *dream job!*" But I'm still not sure as I enter the Bruton building and feel the stares. Why do I need to subject myself to this scrutiny?

When I get to my cube, Alexia the beauty intern is sitting in my seat.

"Oh," she says, looking up and skimming her eyes over my outfit. I'm wearing purple tights, black-heeled triple-strapped Mary Janes, and a fitted black dress cinched with a wide black patent-leather belt—I know I look good, but she gives me a sarcastic "nice outfit" eye roll anyway.

I stand my ground and don't let her appraisal intimidate me. "Can I have my desk, please?" I suddenly realize there's no way I'm going to quit this job and have people like Alexia gossiping about it.

"Of course," she says. "I think Chloe wasn't sure you'd be in today." She stands up and grabs her notebook, sashaying back to the beauty closet where she belongs.

Before I can even get settled, Valentina—the beauty editor—is in my face. "Have you seen Alexia?" she asks.

"Yes," I say. "She was sitting at my desk but I told her I needed it today."

"Oh, right," says Valentina, distractedly looking down the hall through her tortoiseshell-framed glasses. I bet those aren't even prescription.

"So she's probably in the closet now," I say, hoping that Valentina will go away.

She turns her gaze to me. "We weren't sure you'd be back," she says.

Did everyone have some sort of big meeting about the status of my internship? "Why wouldn't I be back?" I ask.

"Well, after the shows last week . . ." she starts. "We just thought maybe you'd—"

"Hole up in my dorm room crying?" I ask angrily, sounding bitchier than I should with a senior editor.

Valentina narrows her eyes at me. "We just weren't sure this was your world anymore," she says flippantly, and then she clicks down the hall on her too-high heels.

I turn to my computer with a frustrated sigh, and I see an e-mail from Marilyn Flynn. It's the first e-mail the editor in chief has ever sent me, so I hurriedly click to open it.

"Come see me when you get in.—MF"

I'm so getting fired from my internship. She sent it at eight-fourteen a.m., and it's now nine forty-two—I must look like a slacker!

I hurriedly grab a notebook and a pen in case she wants me to take story notes. *Please let this be about a story!*

As I start down the corridor toward her office, Chloe pops her head out of her cube and loud-whispers at me. "Violet!"

I turn on my heels. "I have to go see Marilyn Flynn!" I loud-whisper back.

"Come here for one second!" she says, waving me toward her.

"I'm late!" I say, as I tuck into her cube.

"I know," says Chloe. "But I wanted to give you the heads-up. After last week's shows, everyone was talking about you and all the press that was saying you're not model-sized anymore or whatever."

"That's putting it nicely," I say.

"Yeah," says Chloe. "Well, they're jerks." She gives me a sympathetic smile. "Anyway, I pitched that story about you to Marilyn—the one about you going to the health class and how you're a real person with insecurities who's willing to talk to girls like our readers."

"And?" I ask.

"Well, she was leaning toward doing it," says Chloe.

"And now?" I shift my weight as my right heel rubs against the stiff shoe. This pair is so not broken in yet.

"I'm not sure," says Chloe, biting her lip. "She might think now that you're, you know, not with Tryst, that you've lost some of your appeal. Commercially, I mean—not personally."

I stare down at my shoes and hug my notebook tighter into my chest.

"I got a lot of nice messages on MySpace this week," I say, looking up at Chloe.

"Really?" she asks, sounding too surprised.

"Yeah," I say. "Mostly from girls who appreciated seeing me at a different size but still walking the runway . . . a lot of stuff about being a good role model and all that."

"That's great!" says Chloe, as she starts typing rapidly. "Your URL is myspace.com/violetgreenfield, right?"

"Yeah," I say, briefly wondering why she knows that.

"I went on your page when I did the story last year," she says, reading my mind. "Hold on."

She runs out of her cube and returns with five pages of printouts—a bunch of the comments from my page. "Bring these to Marilyn," she says.

"But I don't even know what she wants to—" I start.

"Trust me," Chloe says.

And even though I don't really want to trust the girl who stole Roger from me, I do.

When I tell Marilyn Flynn's assistant that the woman herself called me in this morning, she opens the doors to the editor in chief's office immediately.

The walls are floor-to-ceiling windows with an amazing view of the skyline, and everything in the office is strikingly minimal—a Lucite-topped desk with thin metal legs, a pale white carpet and a black-and-white mod sofa with a low back.

Marilyn Flynn motions for me to sit. She takes a sip of her coffee and then joins me on the couch. I guess she wants to be casual.

"Violet," she says warmly. "How are you doing?"

"I'm fine," I say. "Thank you."

"I'm glad to hear that," she says. "As you may know, Chloe pitched a story about you the other week. Something more than a profile—something about a model who's living beyond the runway and perhaps trying to be a good person, a role model, if you will."

"Yes," I say. "Chloe talked to me about that."

"I'm not sure there's enough bite to this story," she says. "Do you know what I mean by that?"

"Not really," I admit.

"Well, are you still a model?" she asks.

And I'm not sure how to answer. I mean, I'm still me. Still the person who *was* a model, and a pretty successful one. I still have a national ad campaign out in magazines, still get talked about, still could duck under a velvet rope if I wanted to . . . but what does that all mean?

"I don't know," I say.

"I'm aware that you're no longer with Tryst," says Marilyn Flynn.

"Right," I say. The bloggers would have gotten hold of that information.

"And how is the fallout from last week affecting things?" she asks. "I do hope the snark squad isn't getting to you."

I smile. "A little," I say honestly. "But I'm trying to focus on what really matters."

"And what's that, dear?" she asks.

I hand her the printouts Chloe gave me, and I watch her eyes scan the pages.

"I was thinking about the story," I say, as she slowly peruses each message. "And if we do it, maybe it could be less about modeling and more about the universal insecurities we all face. If that means I have to open up a little bit about my own embarrassing memories and dark moments, that's okay with me."

"Why do you want to do that?" she asks.

"Because I have girls who look up to me," I say. "And they need to hear it."

Marilyn Flynn stares at me for a few seconds, like she's trying to see the real intentions behind my words. Maybe she deals with fake types a lot, so she needs to confirm something in a person's eyes.

After what feels like a full minute of silence, she stands up. "Let's do the story," she says.

fifteen

Since Chloe did the profile of "model" me, it's only natural that she'll write this new story. We met to talk about it, and it's not going to totally focus on me—there'll be a few real girls thrown into the mix, but I'm the central person since some readers already know who I am. As much as I've been wary of the spotlight this year, this article feels like something to be proud of, so I'm psyched.

When I'm packing my stuff to leave the city, I'm only slightly sad that I won't see Roger this week. I'm sure he and Chloe have some amazing plan to go to some chic restaurant or a new club or something. But whatever. I've got a semidate with Oliver tonight.

"Ready, Violet?" Chloe wanders over to my cube with her coat on.

"Oh," I say. "I was just going to go back to campus."

"I know," she says. "And I'm coming with you."

"What?" I ask.

"You heard Marilyn—she wants the story by the end of next week." Chloe takes out her lip gloss and starts reapplying it. "That means I need to report it this weekend."

"Oh," I say, not sure how I feel about Chloe coming to Vassar with me. "I hope you don't have to cancel anything special."

"Nah," she says, smiling. "Just a movie night in with Roger. We were going to order Chinese and watch season two of *The Office*."

I force a smile. Somehow hearing about a cozy date like that hurts even more than if they were going out to some fancy party. It makes their relationship seem intimate. It makes it seem more like *mine* and Roger's. *Ouch*.

The train ride to Poughkeepsie is fairly excruciating. Chloe is actually a nice person, I acknowledge, but it's like she's uncomfortable with silence and has to babble and babble to avoid one moment of nonconversation. I learn about her older brother who's a lawyer (snooze), how her parents' divorce made it hard for her to trust guys "until sweet Roger came along" (gag), and how she's always wanted to own a three-legged dog (semi interesting).

"So what are your plans this weekend?" she asks quickly when a silent moment threatens.

"Nothing big," I say. "I do have a date tonight, though."

"Ooh, exciting!" she says, leaning in and grabbing my arm across the seat. "Who is he?"

"This guy Oliver," I say. "I met him in Sociology and he's pretty cool."

She takes out her mini-notebook and starts writing. That's when I know to be careful.

"And what do you like about him?" she asks.

"Well, he listens to what I say," I start. "And he's not about liking me because I'm a model."

"Good reasons," says Chloe. "Will he mind a third wheel with a notebook on your date?"

"It's more like we're meeting at a dorm party," I say. "So I think it'll be fine."

When we finally reach campus, I need a nap. I want to duck into my room for a twenty-minute power rest, but when I get back to the suite, Kurt's flipping through *Vogue* on my bed.

"VV!" he says. "Back from the city tonight? Did you bring me an STD?"

Okay, no power nap. I can't let Kurt's nonsensical joking be on the record.

"He's kidding," I say to Chloe. "Kurt, meet Chloe. She's a reporter for *Teen Fashionista* and they're doing a story that includes a little profile of my normal life."

"Chloe Anderson!" he says, grabbing her hand and kissing it lustily. Kurt has a habit of memorizing the mastheads of the magazines he likes. "A true pleasure."

"K-U-R-T?" Chloe asks.

"Yup," he says. "Last name Allen—A-L-L-E-N."

"Thanks," she says.

"But don't for a second let Violet fool you into thinking she has a normal life!" he says, rushing to the doorway and peeking his head out into the hall. "Did you bring a photographer?" he asks excitedly.

"No," says Chloe. "This piece will be more like a mix of people, so we'll probably just use a portrait of Violet alone."

Kurt pouts for a second, but he recovers quickly. "I guess I'll just give you such colorful quotes that Marilyn Flynn will have to wonder who I am," he says.

"I'm sure that won't be a problem," I say nervously.

"Sit down, curly-q," Kurt says to Chloe. "Has Violet told you about her double love life yet—one here on campus and one in the city?"

I swear I feel my heart stop beating for a moment. My eyes grow to large saucers as I stand behind Chloe and shake my head vigorously *no, no, no, no!*

"Ooh!" squeals Chloe. "Sounds fun!" She poises her pen above her notebook.

Kurt looks up at me quickly, gets it, and doesn't miss a beat.

"Oh, I just mean there's her love for life in the city, and her love for college," he says. "She's very torn. It's hard for her to be a normal girl when she's such a fashion star."

I breathe a sigh of relief. Chloe turns to look back at me.

"Oh," she says, sounding disappointed. "I thought you were going to tell me that Oliver had some competition."

"Did I hear someone say my name?"

I turn to see Oliver standing in the suite doorway. This situation is getting complicated.

"Hi," he says to Chloe, holding out his hand.

"Oliver, meet Chloe," I say. "She's a writer for *Teen Fashionista*."

"She's covering my escapades!" says Kurt.

Chloe laughs. She is so easily charmed.

"I'm actually covering Violet," Chloe says.

"Oh, okay," says Oliver, smiling sincerely.

He looks at me. "Violet—wanna get dinner before we go to the party tonight?"

"Sure," I say, excited that he's asking me on a *real* date in front of Chloe. Maybe she'll tell Roger.

"Great," he says smiling. "My roommate said I could borrow his car, so we can go off campus to the Acrop or something?"

"Ew—the *Acrop*?" Kurt wails, his head snapping up from the magazine he's returned to reading.

"What is that?" I ask.

"The Acropolis is a Poughkeepsie diner," says Kurt. "Really, Oliver, I'd expect you to be more upscale."

Oliver turns red before our eyes, which I find endearing.

"I love diners," I say cheerily. "Nothing like seeing clear color photos of what you're ordering!"

"Okay, cool," he says, slinking out the door. "I'll come by at like eight?"

"Sounds good," I say, closing the door after him. "Kurt! That was so rude!"

"What?" he asks, barely looking up from *Vogue*. "That's a trashy date."

Chloe is scribbling furiously, but I don't see how any of this is relevant to the story. Except the part about me having a date. I peek over her shoulder to see if she's made any notes about Oliver's being cute and tall.

"Violet, I have to go to the bathroom," says Kurt, standing up and grabbing my arm. "Come with?"

"Uh, sure," I say. "Chloe, we'll be right back."

She smiles cheerfully and sits down on our couch.

Kurt almost pulls my arm off in the hallway, and when we get into the bathroom, he folds his arms across his chest and leans back on a sink.

"So . . . " he says. "What's the deal? Why can't Chloe know about Mr. High School Love?"

"No reason," I say, fixing my hair in the mirror so I don't have to look Kurt in the eye. "I just don't want it in print."

"Lies," Kurt says. "You were shaking your head like I was about to tell her you'd killed her grandmother."

"Oh, please," I say, trying to sound casual. "I don't know what you mean."

"Does she know Roger?" Kurt asks. *Damn! Are all gay men this perceptive?*

"I don't know," I say, leaning in to turn on the faucet.

"Why are you washing your hands?" asks Kurt.

"What? Because they're dirty from the train," I say.

"You're nervous," he says. "And it's because you're not being honest with me. But that's okay." He turns off the faucet and hands me a paper towel. "I'll just go ask Chloe if she's ever heard of a boy named Roger."

He starts for the door to the hallway. My heart speeds up and I reach out quickly to grab his elbow.

"Don't," I say, looking down at the dirty tiled floor as he turns back to me. "Chloe is Roger's girlfriend."

On the date with Oliver, I can't concentrate. I'm nervous that Kurt will get drunk later and say something to Chloe at the party. Not because he'll mean to, just because, well, he's Kurt. Subtlety and secrets aren't really his thing.

"Anything besides water?" asks the waiter who sidles up to our booth. Oliver is across the table and Chloe is sitting next to me. She is really starting to bug me—and not just because she's third-wheeling it right now. It's the way she talks in a peppy voice like we're the popular girls in middle school or something, how she writes down absolutely *everything*, how it's *so* easy to make her laugh (that horrible snorting honk).

"Diet Coke," says Chloe.

"Vanilla milkshake," I say. *Take that, calorie counter!*

Oliver gets a beer, and they don't card him. "Impressive," I say.

"It's the dimple," he says, grinning.

Chloe has told us that we should just act like she's not there. She promised to be as quiet as a mouse—as in, she actually used that wording—and yet she can't keep her mouth shut.

"So where are you from, Oliver?" she asks.

"Westport, Connecticut," he says.

I'm not sure I knew which town he was from.

"And do you have any siblings?" asks Chloe.

"Just one—a little sister," he says. "She's fourteen."

Again, not information I've ever requested.

"What's her name?" asks Chloe.

I tune out. *Am I really this self-involved?* I've never asked Oliver about the details of his life. She *is* a reporter, but she's kind of making me feel bad. I should tune back in.

". . . sounds so great!" says Chloe. "Violet has a little brother named Jake who's a star basketball player, so you guys both have awesome siblings."

She smiles at me. I give her a closed-mouth grin, which is all I can muster in the face of such perky energy.

"How did you know about Jake?" I ask.

"Oh, Roger's told me all about you," she says. "Sometimes it seems like his whole life revolved around you back in North Carolina!"

Really? I feel the back of my knees start to sweat.

"Who's Roger?" asks Oliver.

"My boyfriend!" says Chloe, at the same time that I say, "My best friend."

She looks at me and smiles. "I met him through Violet—they've known each other forever."

"That's nice," says Oliver.

"Yeah," says Chloe. "He's a younger man, but he's just so adorable!"

The way her face is glowing makes me want to punch her. But I also want to hear more of what Roger says about me, or about our life in North Carolina. What stories has he told her? What details does he include? Is he smiling when he remembers things about me?

"Violet!" I hear Chloe say loudly.

"Oh, what?" I ask, refocusing on her and Oliver.

"I just told Oliver what I love about Roger, and then he asked you what you look for in a guy," she says.

"Sorry," I say. "I guess my mind was somewhere else."

The party that night is only sort of fun. Oliver is being so nice and paying lots of attention to me, but all I can focus on is Chloe: how she acts, how she talks, how she meets people (with a handshake, which is way too adultlike for a college party). She does manage to worm her way to the front of the keg line a few times, but that's only because she's over twenty-one and she told the hosts she could buy more beer for an after-party.

What is it that Roger likes about her? How can she be the new me when we're so different?

"Your college life is super-fun!" says Chloe, leaning next to me in the window of a room that looks out onto the quad. Campus is really pretty all lit up at night—the sidewalks crisscross in the middle and there are people laughing outside under the streetlamps.

"Yeah," I say halfheartedly, turning away from the window.

"Oliver is sooo sweet!" she chirps. "You should totally bring him into the city for a double date with me and Rog one night."

Rog? Rog?! He never let anyone shorten his name like that.

"You know, it's okay to drink in front of me," Chloe says, nodding at the can of Coke in my hand. "I wouldn't write about it."

"For the record, I'm just not in the mood," I say. And it's true. Though I did think about it and just decided it was best that I not get drunk tonight.

"Do people here know you're a model?" Chloe asks.

"Some," I say, not elaborating. The truth is, I think most people who were at all interested in my being a model at first have now gotten used to seeing me around campus. Maybe I should tell Chloe that so she can quote me, but I really want her to just go away right now, so I'm not encouraging conversation.

"You know, I think you look even prettier when you're not made up for the runway," Chloe says, standing back to appraise me. "You're so put together."

I look down at my dark-wash jeans and loose, light cotton sweat-shirt from American Apparel. My hair is down around my shoulders and I have a dozen silver bangles on my left wrist. Nothing special. Chloe must be drunk.

"So listen," she says when I remain silent. "I was thinking about the rest of the interviews I need, and I'm hoping you'll come back into the city with me tomorrow."

"I have some studying to do," I say curtly. "Why do you need me to come?"

"I want to get you in all your environments, with all your close friends," she says. "I called Roger and he's up for hanging out to-morrow night. I'm hoping you can get in touch with your old room-mates Veronica and Sam to see if they can meet us too. Then I'll have high school world, college world, and modeling covered. That should satisfy Marilyn."

"I guess," I say, not seeing a way to say no.

"Great!" says Chloe. "We can take a late train so we can sleep in—I'm sure I'll have a *monster* hangover!"

I give her a thin smile. It's lame when people talk about how much they're drinking, especially while they're still drinking.

When she leaves me to refill her cup, Oliver comes over.

"Is that Chloe chick going to be around all night?" he asks. I can tell he's drunk by his use of the word *chick*—Oliver is usually very Vassar-PC about referring to women.

"I think so," I say.

"So all our actions will be recorded for the *Teen Fashionista* audience?" he asks.

"It's possible," I say.

"I guess we can have a real date another time, then?" he asks, looking hopeful.

"Sure," I say, hoping that he won't notice that I'm smiling with my mouth but not my eyes.

The next morning, there's a knock on my door. I look at the clock—nine forty-three a.m.

"Kurt, go back to bed!" I shout. But it's muffled in my pillow.

"What?" asks Chloe, fully dressed and smiling brightly as she opens my door to peek in. "I brought you coffee!"

I sit up and brush the hair out of my eyes. "Um, thanks," I say. "What happened to the late train?"

"This *is* the late train!" she says, coming into my room and sitting down on my bed. I really need to get a chair in here. "Besides, I couldn't sleep this morning. I got so excited about the story, Violet. I really think it's going to be great."

My mind runs through last night: date with Oliver where Chloe talked his ear off, totally sober at the party, in bed by two a.m. How is this a great story?

"Did you sleep okay?" I ask.

"Oh, yeah," she says. "The couch is so comfortable! And after sharing a tiny dorm bed or my old twin with Roger most nights, it was nice to have some room to spread out."

Ick! I want to cover my ears with my hands and sing *Lalalalalalalala.* But that might look weird. Instead I change the subject.

"I talked to Veronica last night," I say. "She's in for tonight, and she'll call Sam."

"Fantastic!" says Chloe. "Roger's going to meet us for lunch before we go out with everyone else. That's why we need to catch the eleven thirty-three train. Think you can get ready quickly?"

The extent to which Chloe is annoying me is growing by the minute. Now I'm supposed to get out of bed *early* on a Saturday so we can play *Three's Company* with Roger all afternoon?

"Sure," I say. I'm such a wimp.

When I get to the shower, I'm surprised to hear "Like a virgin— ooh!" coming from the second stall. I haven't had a run-in with the shower-hookup hallmates in a while, and I'm almost totally comfortable with this same-sex bathroom thing. Besides, I recognize this singing voice.

I step into my shower and start shampooing before I yell over to Kurt. "Why are you up so early?" I ask.

"VV!" he trills back, his voice echoing off the tiled walls. "I hear we're catching the eleven thirty-three train, that's why!"

"We?" I ask, rinsing the suds from my hair.

"*Oui!*" he says with a French accent. "Chloe Anderson invited me last night."

"She did?" I ask. Kurt behaved himself at the party, but having him hang out with me, Roger, and Chloe while he knows the backstory doesn't seem wise. I'm about to tell him he absolutely can't come when I hear him singing, *"I get to meet Veronica Tra-ask, I get to meet Veronica Tra-ask . . ."* He sounds so excited.

"Couldn't you come up later and meet us out tonight?" I ask. "I mean, you probably have a lot of reading and stuff to do."

I hear his shower shut off. "And miss the afternoon with Roger?" he asks. "Not a chance in hell, pretty princess."

I poke my head out from my shower curtain. "Promise me you won't say a word," I say. "Or even roll your eyes or *anything!* Roger is really good at reading people so he'll know if you're acting weird."

"Do you think I don't know how to behave?" he asks, feigning offense.

I shrug my naked shoulders behind the curtain.

"I, Violet Greenfield, am a drama student!" he says. "And don't worry. I'll put on quite a show."

He grabs his toiletry bag and walks out into the hall with just a towel around his waist.

That's what I'm afraid of, I think.

sixteen

When our train finally reaches Grand Central, I'm feeling more rested. Kurt and Chloe chattered the whole ride down, which was a relief—I got some iPod time in once I determined that Kurt was going to stick to safe subjects and not really talk about Roger.

I note with satisfaction that Roger isn't at the station to meet Chloe like he met me that one time. Kurt and I have our overnight bags—I've arranged for us to spend the night at Aunt Rita's in Brooklyn—and we stop by Chloe's apartment to drop them off so we won't have to carry them to lunch.

Her tiny studio is adorable, I have to admit. There's a full bathroom with a window and little dressing room nook, as well as a semi-separate kitchen next to the living room/bedroom area. She has all the walls painted pastel shades, which could turn out Easter egg, but she's done it really well. There are fresh flowers on the entry table, and I notice that all the makeup on her vanity is super-high-end. Someone's been raiding the *Teen Fashionista* beauty closet.

"Ooh! A Murphy bed!" says Kurt, pointing to the part of the wall that folds down at night and becomes her sleeping area.

I imagine Roger here, hanging out and cooking dinner, cuddling with her on the small wall-bed as they watch TV.

"Is this Roger?!" Kurt exclaims, holding up a photo he's plucked from the bookshelf. I lean over his shoulder to peek. It's one of those annoying him-holding-her-from-behind photos. Even worse, it's black-and-white and it looks like it was taken on top of the Empire State Building. *Retch*.

"Yeah," says Chloe, her smile growing.

"He's way hotter here than in the old photos Violet has in her room," Kurt says to Chloe. Then he turns to me. "Violet, you didn't tell me they grew hipster boys like these in North Carolina. Might be time for a hometown visit!"

"They're all in gay denial," I say.

"I can fix that," says Kurt, with a glint in his eye. Having him with us is actually turning out to be a good thing. It's hard to be in a bad mood with Kurt around.

"So where are we meeting Mr. Wonderful?" asks Kurt.

"At a café in the West Village," says Chloe. "It's close. And it's Roger's favorite."

I hate that she knows his favorite spot in New York and I don't.

From Chloe's Chelsea apartment, we walk ten blocks downtown until we're in the twisting and weaving streets of the West Village. The numbers stop having the grid significance they have in other parts of Manhattan, which is part of why the streets in this neighborhood are so Euro-pretty. It kind of reminds me of Paris, though I don't say that out loud—it would sound snooty.

We reach a small corner café with lace curtains in the windows and a giant pastry counter.

"Are you *sure* he's not gay?" asks Kurt.

I punch him in the arm.

"It's Roger's favorite because he says it reminds him of Barcelona," explains Chloe.

My heart flip-flops. Barcelona is where Roger and I traveled together last year. I wonder if that's why he loves this place.

I look around and see shiny silver napkin holders and tiny, nubby candles on each of the tables, along with bud vases with single pink roses in them. It's completely charming.

Then I see Roger at a table by the window. For a moment, when he looks at me, it's like just the two of us are meeting. Just the two of us in a world where we can tuck into a corner and talk for hours.

And then I hear Chloe's high-pitched voice. "Baby!" she squeals. She rushes into the seat next to Roger and plants a kiss on his lips. Kurt and I settle in across from them, and he squeezes my hand under the table. It's nice to have his sympathy.

"Roger, this is Kurt," says Chloe, when she's done sucking his face. "He's Violet's friend from Vassar."

"Charmed," says Kurt, holding out his hand like he wants Roger to kiss it. Roger laughs and shakes it awkwardly.

"Bummer," says Kurt softly. Then, louder, "Nice to meet you."

"You too," says Roger.

Chloe takes out her mini–tape recorder and puts it on the table. We all stare at it and feel suddenly awkward.

"This place is really cute," I say, looking up at Roger. "Chloe says it's your favorite?"

"Yeah," says Roger. "Remember that open-air café we stopped at for lunch in Barcelona?"

"On Las Ramblas near the flower vendors and musicians," I say.

"Right—the one with the paper tablecloths and silver napkin holders," says Roger.

"Just like this place," I say, smiling. We grin at each other for a moment and I can feel my face start to get warm.

"I love Barcelona," chirps Chloe. The warm feeling subsides quickly. "I spent six months there as a junior in college, you know. Did Roger tell you?"

"No," I say.

"It's such a romantic city," she says, looking over at Roger.

"It is," Roger says, looking at me.

Kurt coughs. "So what's good here?" he asks. "I'm starving!"

Later that night, we have plans to meet Veronica and Sam at Marquee. This is so not my scene anymore, but Chloe thinks that we should work my old roommates into the feature, and that's where they're going tonight.

"It's DJ-model night," explains Veronica. "The press will be out in full force."

She's on a mission to land her next campaign, to walk fashion's most prestigious runways, to book the cover of *Vogue*. That world seems so far away to me now.

When we get to the door, I lead everyone to a back entrance and the bouncer gives me a hug. "Hey, pretty lady," he says. "How many?"

"Four," I say. "Thanks."

Kurt is springing up and down with excitement as we head to the corner booth where I know Sam and Veronica will be. There are a couple of other models sitting with them, but Veronica boots those girls when she sees us coming. She's always been kind of a bitch like that.

She cheek-kisses Roger and Chloe, and gives me a real hug. Then she turns to Kurt.

He looks like he's standing in the presence of God or something. His mouth is wide open and his hands are shaking.

"You're my favorite," he screams over the pulsating music.

"Traitor!" I shout, totally joking. Sam feigns offense too before leaning over the table to greet Kurt with a cheek smooch.

Veronica laughs and kisses the other cheek. He puts his hand up to the spot where her lips were and leaves it there for a full minute.

"So we're on the record tonight?" Veronica loud-whispers to me when we sit down together in the booth.

"Yeah," I say. "Good thing no one can hear each other or we'd have to be really careful."

Chloe and Roger squeeze in on one side, and Sam sits on the edge so Kurt can be next to Veronica, who's next to me in the middle. He still looks like a starstruck toddler staring at Elmo.

We grab glasses from the waiter and pour the bottle of champagne that's chilling by the table.

"Oh, yeah. This is how we do it," says Kurt.

"No it's not!" I laugh, thinking about how we're usually downing cans of Busch Light in my dorm room.

A remix of that eighties song "Bizarre Love Triangle" comes on and Kurt gives me a meaningful look. Then he grabs my hand. "Let's dance!"

He pulls Veronica and Sam out onto the floor, too, and I can tell this is his totally Studio 54 fantasy, being in the middle of three models on a black light–lit dance floor. If only some amazingly ripped waiter would notice him and slip a number into his pocket, Kurt would be in heaven.

We dance for a few more songs, but when eighties remixes give way to hard-core house music, I have to bow out. I head back to the booth to find Roger and Chloe arguing.

". . . not helping your story!" Roger is saying.

"It is too!" yells Chloe.

"Please!" shouts Roger. "You just want a big night out because you're tired of me not getting into clubs with you. Well guess what: I don't even *like* clubs! And I'm *glad* I can't get in without Violet— she's the only thing that makes these places halfway bearable."

The both look up to see me staring at them. I'm being a totally obvious eavesdropper because I had to lean in to hear them, even though they were screaming at each other.

Chloe grabs her clutch and storms out onto the dance floor, where I watch her join Kurt, Veronica, and Sam. She looks like a munchkin because they're all so tall, but she starts dancing like she's having the time of her life.

I look back at Roger and give him a shrug.

"You wanna get out of here?" he asks.

"Yeah," I say.

He grabs my hand and we head for the back exit.

It's freezing outside, but I feel exhilarated and warm as Roger pulls me down the block, not letting go of my hand.

"What was that all about?" I ask when we've walked to Eighth Avenue, which is just past the no-man's-land club zone farther west.

"Nothing," says Roger, releasing his grip. "I don't want to talk about it."

"Okay," I say, sticking my hands into my coat pockets. I spot a chalkboard sign with the words *Cheese Fries* written on it in big yellow letters. I look up at Roger at the exact moment he sees the sign.

He meets my eyes and says, "Yes!"

We walk into an old English-style pub with brass beer taps and a giant jukebox in the corner. There are three guys drinking at the bar, but lots of empty tables.

"You get the fries, I'll get the music," says Roger.

The bartender is wearing a patch over one eye, and I'm nervous for a second that he'll card me, but he doesn't. I order a plate of cheese fries and two pints of Stella, which is what I saw this really cool British model drink in Paris once.

I sit down next to Roger's coat while he finishes picking out music. I already know that I'll read into every word of every song, because I'm a dork like that. I wonder if he knows too.

When he gets to the table, the bartender is already bringing out the cheese fries.

"Thanks," I say. He gives me a wink with the visible eye.

"One-Eyed Willie has a crush on you," says Roger.

"These cheese fries aren't quite as good as—" I start.

"The ones at Linda's," Roger finishes. At this bar Linda's in Chapel Hill, the cheese fries come with bits of bacon and chives and delicious ranch dressing. These are pretty plain.

"Yeah, New Yorkers just don't know the joy of ranch dressing and Bac-Os bits like we do," I say, twirling a fry in the air to catch the dripping cheese.

"At least they got a good melt going," says Roger.

"True," I say. "How's the jukebox?" The song that just came on is John Cougar Mellencamp's "Small Town," which I am positive is *not* Roger's pick.

"Not so awful that I have to pick Cougar," Roger says, taking a swill of his Stella. "This is good beer!"

"Yeah, it beats Busch Light," I say, already feeling a little giddy from the few sips I've taken.

We smile at each other, and I'm wondering how we got here. Two best friends who've been close since we were toddlers, sitting in a warm bar on a New York City winter night in front of a glowing jukebox and two pints.

"This is so much better than that club," says Roger, reading my mind.

"Totally," I say. "Whenever I'm at a club, I feel like I'm *supposed* to like it, like I should be having fun, but I never really am."

"Exactly!" Roger says, sounding angry. He looks down at the table.

"Are you upset?" I ask.

"No," he says, his eyes softening as he looks up at me. "Not anymore."

My heart jumps a little when he reaches out his hand. I almost think he's going to grab my wrist, but instead he picks up my beer. "Let's down these?" he asks, eyes sparkling.

"Go!" I shout, grabbing my glass and racing to finish the pint. I almost beat him.

The pirate bartender comes over instantly. "Another round?" he asks.

"Yes," I say, breathless.

A few beers later, Roger and I are arguing about the merits of *Gossip Girl* (good) verses *The Hills* (better).

"*The Hills* is *real!*" I say. "How can you argue for fiction over real drama?!"

"What the hell are you talking about?!" says Roger with a look of disbelief. "*The Hills* is about as real as an episode of *All My Children*."

"You're just a *Gossip Girl* fan because you imagine yourself as Dan Humphrey," I say.

"Do you deny that I have a certain Penn Badgley quality?"

Roger asks, his head tilted and his doofy Original Penguin sweater all rumpled from the hand gestures he's been making while arguing with me.

"I guess I see a little PB in you," I say, laughing. "But that show's so over-the-top anyway."

"It still defines high school, does it not?" he asks.

"Someone else's high school maybe," I say.

"Like Veronica's," says Roger. "Could you believe she just kicked out those other models when we got there?"

"That's so her," I say. "At least you're reaping the rewards of her fearless social hierarchy."

"You've been a good friend to her," he says.

"I guess," I say. "I'm not sure what we have in common since I've quit modeling though. I talk to her less and less."

"Like when Jenny Glassman stopped being your friend in first grade because you quit ballet?" asks Roger.

"Sort of," I say. "Except we're not six years old."

"Still, you should stay in touch with Veronica," says Roger. "It'll mean a lot to her someday."

"Thanks, wise man," I say, smiling.

I love this. I love Roger giving me advice and really listening to what I say. I love that he can reference first grade to get his point across, I love that he *knows* me. I'm about to try tell him how much I love this—how much I love *us*—when I hear the first strains of a familiar song.

"Your pick?" I look Roger in the eyes.

"Do you have to ask?" he says.

It's "All I Want Is You," the U2 song. I remember the first time I heard it—it was on a mix CD Roger's cool older cousin Frank made him when we were around twelve. Frank always made the *best* mixes with retro songs I never heard anywhere else. I would kill to copy that guy's iPod playlists.

"You say you want

Diamonds on a ring of gold . . ."

We used to listen to it over and over when we were in middle school. I'd always be picturing Brian Radcliff, my popular-guy crush of like five years. Roger would pick a different girl to focus on every few weeks, but I always got the feeling he wasn't that into any of them.

We sit in silence, listening to Bono sing as the bartender starts to turn the chairs upside-down onto the tables, as the guy from the kitchen comes out to sweep the floor, as the three men who were at the bar shuffle to the door.

"I guess we should go," says Roger, standing up and holding out his hand for me as Bono screams the last "All I want is yoo-uu"s of the song.

"We'll miss your other songs," I protest.

"It's probably best," says Roger.

"Okay," I say, not really wanting to leave the warmth of this bar where no one else exists, where it's just us, where I almost told Roger . . .

"I love you." I hear my voice but it seems like it's not attached to me. *Did I just say that?*

"What?" asks Roger. "Say that again?"

"No," I say, standing up without taking his hand.

"No?" he asks. "You won't say it again?"

"I don't even know what I was saying," I stammer, realizing as I stand up that I'm a little tipsier than I anticipated. "I think I'm drunk." I hold my hand up to my forehead with a grimace, hoping I didn't just say what I think I said.

"So you didn't mean what you said?" Roger asks, looking at me quizzically.

"I thought you didn't hear me," I say.

"I heard you," he says, staring at my face but not really looking in my eyes. He doesn't look happy.

I want to say something else, like how I didn't really understand what was important to me until now, how I think I've loved him for a long time without knowing it.

But he speaks first. "Come on, we should go."

We walk to the door without looking at each other.

This time, when the two of us step out into the winter air, it feels much colder than before.

seventeen

When we get back to Marquee, I can see Chloe's blond curls bouncing up and down as she staggers on the sidewalk. Kurt is holding her up.

"Hey, guys," Roger says.

Chloe lunges at him affectionately, wrapping her arms around his shoulders and almost taking him down. "I'm sorry, baby," she slurs. "I love you."

"Let's get you home," says Roger. He reaches out to shake Kurt's hand. "See you later, man. Thanks for watching her."

He hails a cab and helps Chloe into the backseat. Then he stands up and looks at me before climbing in.

"Good night, Violet," he says.

I wave halfheartedly. I'm not quite sure what just happened, but I'm feeling infinitely sad.

As soon as the taxi drives away, Kurt whirls around on me. "Where *were* you for the last four hours?!" he asks. Before I can answer, though, he starts talking animatedly. "Ooh, you are *lucky* that Chloe got tanked! She hardly noticed that *both* you and Roger were missing, thanks to all the champagne Veronica and Sam were feeding her. You so owe us!"

I look down at my cell phone and see that I missed six calls. *Oops.* "The bar was loud," I say, as I notice that it's four twenty-six a.m. "Did Veronica and Sam leave?"

"Yeah," says Kurt. "They both have early call times tomorrow."

"Look at you, talking like an industry insider," I say, punching Kurt on the shoulder.

"Owww," he whines. "I'm delicate."

"Let's get a cab," I say. "My treat. The trains take forever this time of night."

"Okay, Miss New York City," he says.

When we get to Rita's in Brooklyn, I locate the hidden key underneath a flowerpot, which is completely obvious but that's how Rita is. We tiptoe downstairs and find the guest bedroom—still with Raggedy Ann and Andy dolls, one on each bed—ready for us.

"I get Andy!" whispers Kurt.

"Of course," I say. I brush my teeth, take out my contacts, wash my face, and put on an old T-shirt I like to sleep in. I try to forget what I said to Roger—I don't want to think about it. At least until the sun comes up.

I wake to the smell of pancakes, which is totally unusual. I'd expect Rita to *maybe* leave us some stale granola in the cupboards and a note that says she'll see us later.

I look over at Kurt's bed. It's completely made up with Raggedy Andy sitting front and center, like no one even slept there. I hate being the last one awake.

I pull on jeans, grab my glasses from my bag, and walk upstairs without brushing my hair. When I get to the kitchen, I see Aunt Rita sitting at the table, beaming, while Kurt works a frying pan over the gas stove's flame. He's actually flipping a pancake in the air and catching it.

"Oh, Violet!" Rita clasps her hands together when she sees me. "Kurt is just wonderful!"

I give her a smirk and look over at Kurt. "When did you learn to cook like a circus clown?" I ask, pulling out a chair at the table and sitting down.

"Gay boys in high school don't have much of a social life in my hometown," he says. "I improvised by spending time with my Food Network friends."

Rita laughs uproariously. I haven't seen her this distracted from her Sunday paper since the day I came home from a club and my photo was on Page Six in the *New York Post*. There's so much sunshine in this room—and the pancakes smell so good as Kurt puts a plate in front of me—that I almost forget I completely humiliated myself last night.

I don't know why I had to go and say those three words to Roger. And the way he reacted? So cold, so uncaring—like he didn't want to hear it at all. I guess I didn't think he'd leave Chloe and book a flight to Hawaii with me, but a tender smile would have been nice!

"Why are you frowning at your blueberry pancake?" asks Kurt. "If you tell me you don't like blueberries I'm going to spatula the side of your head!"

"It's not that," I say, with a heavy sigh.

"Uh-oh," says Rita. "I know that sound. What's the heartache about?"

And for some reason, maybe because I've really grown to trust Rita over the past year, or maybe because I feel like I can confide in

Kurt, or maybe just because I'm tired of carrying my feelings inside and denying them for so long, I just say it plainly: "I told Roger that I loved him last night."

Silence. I can hear the hum of the refrigerator and the sizzle of butter in Kurt's pan as he pauses and looks up at me from the stove.

Then Rita reaches over and covers my hand with hers. I imagine she's going to pat it condescendingly and tell me it'll all be okay. Instead, she lifts my hand into the air and yells, "Hallelujah! It's about time!"

Kurt gives a "whoop!" on impulse, and I start to smile in spite of myself.

"What?" I ask Rita, confused by her enthusiasm.

"Violet, I've known that you and that boy were made for each other since I saw him share his chocolate ice cream cone with you in the second grade," she says. "For a seven-year-old, giving up ice cream is love."

"That's stupid," I say, frowning down at the scuffed wooden table. "Besides, he didn't say it back. He wouldn't even look at me after I said it."

"Really?" asks Kurt, giving me an *ouch* face.

"Yeah, really," I say.

"Oh, that doesn't matter," says Rita. "Point is, you said it. You told him! Don't you feel great?!"

"No," I say. "I feel stupid. I feel rejected. I feel awful."

"Yeesh, Debbie Downer," says Kurt.

I give him the evil eye.

"Violet, honey, lighten up," says Rita. "You and Roger will be okay. This I know for sure."

"You sound like Oprah," I say, unconvinced.

"Trust me," she says, squeezing my arm affectionately. "Have I ever steered you wrong?"

I refrain from mentioning the time she offered me pot when I was twelve. In general, she's been a pretty upstanding aunt.

"Forget it," I say. "It's not a big deal."

Kurt and Rita go back to their pancake banter, and I smile at the appropriate moments and answer my aunt's questions about how school's going.

But when I said it wasn't a big deal that Roger gave me the cold shoulder last night, I was lying. The truth is, it means *everything*.

eighteen

Kurt and I ride the train back to Vassar that afternoon, and although he tries to steer the conversation toward Roger and what happened last night, it's easy enough to distract him by asking about Gregory Danner and how their relationship is going. Sometimes a certain level of self-involvement is good in a friend.

Veronica calls while I'm climbing the stairs to the third floor, but when she asks me where Roger and I went, I pretend like we just got food and it was no big deal. I can tell she's distracted—she's on set for *Nylon* doing a photo shoot celebrating the iconic fashion of Debbie Harry from Blondie, whom she's always adored—so I don't really want to get into the drama.

Back in my room, I look up at the mirror, almost forgetting that the poem from Las Ramblas isn't going to be there, that I already put it away and declared myself over it. Over New York City, over the modeling world, and over Roger. I should have remembered that when we were in a warm bar downing pints of Stella.

I log on to myspace.com/violetgreenfield and write a poem about my feelings. Roger will make fun of that if he sees it, but somehow it makes me feel better. Besides, I've noticed that lots of other MySpace bloggers post poetry, and some of it isn't bad.

I have the urge to curl up in bed and feel sorry for myself, but I don't want to be that girl anymore. I grab a towel and head for the bathroom to take a long, hot shower. When I come back to my room, I put on the honeysuckle-scented lotion that smells like summers in North Carolina. I grab a black Tibi shift dress that I bought at Anthropologie and put on the silver ballet flats that fit my feet just right. I brush my hair out and blow it dry a little so that it has that shampoo commercial look. I put on some lip stain and a swipe of mascara.

Then I go down to check my mail.

Sure enough, Oliver is working a late afternoon shift. Sunday is the day when the student workers catch up on distributing any overflow of mail from the week. I'm crossing my fingers for a package slip, so that I *have* to go up to the post office window and talk to him, but when I open the small metal door to my box, all I see are two magazines and a letter from my mom. I can already tell what's in the Mom letter—a color photocopied collage.

My mom always does this. Instead of making reprints of photos like a normal person, she takes them to Kinko's and just photocopies old pictures onto heavy-stock paper. It's a little lame, but also sweet. I open it over the trash can in the College Center, expecting to see some silly shot of Jake and my dad playing basketball in the driveway. Her note says, "I hope your new friends in college are as wonderful as your friends from home. XOXO, Mom."

I'm about to pull out the photos when I sense someone looking over my shoulder.

"Hey," I hear in my ear. I spin around to see Oliver's eyes less than a foot from my face.

"Hi," I say.

We stare at each other, unsure what comes next.

"You've been in the city a lot," he finally says.

"Well, just this weekend for that magazine story," I say, and I feel like I can't really look in his eyes, so I stare past him at the ATM line on the far wall.

"Right," he says.

"But I'm around now," I say, smiling and focusing on him. "Wanna go off campus for dinner?"

Did I just ask Oliver out? Whoa. I'd feel immediately embarrassed if it weren't for the huge grin spreading across his face.

"Okay," he says. "The Dutch for Mexican?"

I'm supposed to meet Oliver in front of Main Building at seven p.m., and but it's six fifty-eight and Kurt is still arguing with me.

"Explain to me again why you're going on a date with your second-choice boy," he says, emptying my bureau drawers as he looks for a tight T-shirt to borrow.

"He's not my second choice," I say. "He's my first choice of guys who are *available*."

"Nice spin," says Kurt, standing up and holding an extra-long navy blue C&C California shirt up to his chest. "But I don't think you should be doing this. Your time would be better spent figuring out how to break up Roger and Chloe."

"Ugh—you sound like Veronica." I groan.

"Veronica Trask?" He smiles. "Why, thank you!"

"I *have* to go," I say. "I asked *him*!"

"Okay, okay," says Kurt, waving his hands like he's done with this conversation. He holds up the shirt again and walks to the full-length mirror behind the door. "But first tell me—am I a navy blue boy?"

The Dutch Cabin is this restaurant/bar that's just across the street from campus. It's all dark wood and low lighting, and although it doesn't sound like a Mexican place, they have great burritos.

"Did you have fun in the city?" asks Oliver.

Bad topic. Divert! Divert!

"It was okay," I say. "So are you doing anything cool for break?"

Spring break is coming up—we have two weeks off—so everyone's planning all these big trips to the beach with their friend groups. Kurt, Fan, and Jess are spending a week at Jess's mom's beach house in New Jersey. They invited me, but Marilyn Flynn also asked if I could work at *Teen Fashionista* during spring break—like full-time Monday through Friday—and, being passive old me, I had trouble saying no. Rita already said I can stay with her in Brooklyn.

"Just going home to hang out with Taylor," he says.

"Taylor?" I ask, wondering if he's talking about an ex-girlfriend.

"My little sister," he says. "Remember we talked about her that night at the diner with Chloe?"

"Oh, right," I say, trying to disguise the fact that I have no memory of his sister's name because I was in Roger-daydream-land that whole night.

"She's a great kid," he says. "I mean, she's a freshman in high school so she's not really a kid, but she'll always be younger so I think of her that way, you know?"

"Yeah," I say, picking at the chips in the middle of the table.

"Is that how you feel about Jake?" he asks.

He remembered my brother's name. More guilt. "Sort of," I say. "But with Jake it's like he's always seemed older than me in some ways."

"How so?" asks Oliver, leaning in and looking genuinely interested.

"He played sports, so he got kind of naturally popular in middle school," I say. "And he knew people in my grade and stuff."

"Did you play any sports?" asks Oliver.

"Nope," I say, smiling at the idea of my clumsy self doing anything coordinated. "I was more like a wallflower."

"That's hard to believe," he says.

"It's true," I say, thinking about all the times I watched Shelly Ryan walk down the hall with the Bee's Knees girls—the ruling popular crowd at my school. It seems like a hundred years ago.

Oliver dips a chip into the chunky tomato salsa and holds it up to my mouth like he wants to feed it to me.

Weird! This is not a move I like, but I bite into the chip to keep from making the moment more awkward. It breaks in half and some salsa falls on the table. I laugh and wipe it up with my napkin. *Who's into other people feeding them?*

"I bet *someone* noticed you in high school," says Oliver, dipping another chip and mercifully putting it in his own mouth.

"Someone did," I say, suppressing a sigh. I smile so that I won't look sad.

And suddenly it doesn't matter that this is my first real date with Oliver, because no matter how kind he's been or how many times he earnestly flashes that dimple, he's still not the one in my heart. (And not just because of the feeding-me thing.)

After dinner, we head to a low-key on-campus party, which is pretty much what we do every weekend, even on Sunday. We get in line for the keg, drink a few beers, and talk to whomever we recognize from our classes. Kurt and Jess are there, so I join them in the hallway when Oliver spots some of his newspaper friends.

"Hey," I say, bumping Jess's hip from behind.

"How's your date going?" she asks. "Are you over what's-his-name yet?"

I glare at Kurt.

"We're all friends here, right?" he says. "Friends need to know stuff. Besides, you told Fan already!"

"Don't be mad at Kurt," says Jess. "I've noticed your mood swings lately, and I was just asking questions until I got an answer that made sense."

"I'm sure he cracked in all of thirty seconds," I say, but I'm smiling. I trust Jess.

"So is Oliver back in the number one slot?" Kurt asks.

"He fed me," I say, knowing this will explain things.

"Wait, like food to mouth?" asks Jess, wrinkling her nose.

"Yes," I say. "It was super-weird."

"And Roger would never feed you," says Kurt.

"Not in a million years," I say.

"Well, there you go," says Kurt. "I mean you *have* to find someone who knows that feeding is unacceptable."

Jess laughs. They're joking, but I can tell they know what I mean. It's not one thing, it's just a general feeling of "Does this person *get* me?" With Roger that's never a question I have to ask.

"So you told him you want to just be friends?" asks Jess.

Then I see Oliver heading down the hallway toward us. "Not yet," I whisper.

When he gets close, Oliver puts his arms around me, and I see Kurt raise his eyebrows.

"Hi," Oliver says softly. I can tell he just chugged a few beers—

this is a bold move for him. And when he leans in to kiss me, I want to feel that flutter of excitement. It's not like I feel *nothing*—he does have great lips and his arms fit perfectly around my waist as he pulls me in. But he's drunk and I'm sober and my mind is a thousand miles away. He doesn't seem to notice, though, as his tongue probes my mouth.

I put my hand on his chest and push him back gently. "We're in public," I say.

"Want to go to my room?" he asks.

I shake my head no. He smiles and mouths *okay* before he works his way back to the keg. He doesn't realize that I'm not just saying no right now—I'm saying no for good.

I leave the party early and go back to my room. I know Fan's studying for a midterm, so it'll be quiet and I'll have a chance to catch up on work too. It *is* Sunday night, and with all this back and forth to the city, I'm not exactly keeping up with a hundred percent of my reading. Still, I'm doing okay in my classes, and I've only got two real midterms coming up—there isn't one for Creative Writing, and there's just a paper for Sociology, which I think will be easier than a test. I've always liked being evaluated on writing more than yes-or-no questions.

I notice the envelope from my mom sitting on my desk, and I realize that I forgot to open it. I pull out the sheet of paper slowly, and I see a collage of old photos. It's me and Julie at the neighborhood pool in the summer before sixth grade, me and Roger on our bikes in the snow the year when we both got ten-speeds and it was a white Christmas for the first time in like a decade, the three of us sticking out our tongues for a self-taken shot just before junior year of high school . . . it's covered with memories. When I look at the shot of me and Roger at the prom less than a year ago, my heart sinks. He looks so happy, and I do too, I realize. Why didn't I know then that we were perfect for each other? Why couldn't I see past our friendship to something bigger, something that I want more than anything now?

I pick up the phone and call Julie.

"Hey!" she says.

"How are you?" I ask.

"Ugh," she grunts. "Midterms are keeping me in total solitude in my room. I'm slaving over Aristotle's metaphysics theories."

"Sounds smart," I say.

"Yeah, if I could understand half of what he wrote," she says. "So what's up?"

"I don't know," I say, sighing.

"V, it's me," says Julie. "Spill." And I stare down at her sixth-grade face on the collage my mom sent, so grateful that she's *still* listening to me whine.

"I told Roger I loved him," I say, quickly so I won't back out.

"You *what?!*" she screams so loudly that I have to pull the phone away from my ear for a sec.

"I was drunk," I say. "He put 'All I Want Is You' on the jukebox! It was coercion."

"Wait—back up," says Julie, returning to normal volume but still sounding intense. "Whole-story time."

So I tell her about the bar night, and how I've been wanting to tell Roger how I feel since the night I left Paris.

"I knew it," she says. "I could tell when we were home over Christmas."

"Well, whatever," I say. "He totally cold-fished me. He could hardly look at me after I said it."

"Don't you think maybe it was hard for him to hear?" asks Julie.

"What do you mean?" I ask.

"Well, duh—he's dating someone," she says. "And also, you've been pretty much blowing him off for like ten years."

"I wasn't blowing him off!" I say. "I just didn't know—"

"Please, Violet," Julie interrupts. "Somewhere inside you knew. There's no way you couldn't have."

I think back to all the times I caught Roger looking at me in the passenger-side mirror of Julie's car, when he'd smile at me for a little too long after we shared a laugh, and when his hugs were extra-tight and he wouldn't let go.

"Okay, maybe I subconsciously knew," I admit. "But that's not the point."

"So what is the point?" asks Julie. "That your timing is off because Chloe got there first?"

"I guess," I say, feeling more bummed than I was before I called Julie. Isn't she supposed to make me feel better?

"Well, I've always known that Roger's your real Funny Monkey," says Julie, using our code term for *soul mate*. I look over on my bed and see Funny Monkey smirking at me.

"If this were a movie, there would be a knock at the door right now," I say.

"Right," says Julie. "And Roger would take you in his arms and kiss you and tell you Chloe was out of the picture."

"Yup," I say, sighing.

And then, a knock.

"Jules!" I say. "A knock!"

"Go, go!" she says. "Call me back, though."

"Okay." I flip my phone shut and look in the mirror to make sure my hair is okay. I even swipe on some lip gloss, though I know it's probably just Jess forgetting her keys or something. I am a sucker for potential movie moments.

I open the door and see his pensive eyes.

"Hi, Oliver," I say, surprised at how truly disappointed I feel.

"Hey," he says, his face relaxing. "Can I come in?"

"Sure," I say. I plop down on the couch to make it clear we won't be heading into my bedroom. He sits down beside me.

"So you jetted out of the party," he says. He seems to have sobered up a bit.

"Yeah, I had some work to do," I say.

"I thought we were sort of on a date," he says.

"So I was supposed to check in with you or something?" I ask, sounding meaner than I want to.

"No," he says, turning his head to face the wall in front of us. He leans over with his elbows on his knees and looks down at the floor.

"Sorry," I say, softening my harsh tone. It's not Oliver's fault that he's not my Funny Monkey. "I just felt like I should go."

"Was it because I did a keg stand?" he asks, looking up at me. "Because if it was that, then I will totally relinquish that behavior. I mean, it hurt and wasn't that fun anyway—"

"It's not the keg stand," I say.

"Then what is it?" he asks, looking at me seriously. "I thought maybe we had something starting here . . . Did you just suddenly stop liking me?"

I look down at my fingers and study the purple polish that's flaking off in tiny spots on each nail. I can feel Oliver's breath beside me as he waits for me to explain myself.

"It's someone else," I say. I look up and see him flinch a little bit.

"Oh," he says quietly.

And there's this moment between us, when I know he's hurt and I'm the reason, where I consider saying, *But it's nothing, and I really do like you, so let's go out again sometime.* But I stay quiet, because I know that wouldn't help things—it would just put off this painful interaction.

"High school boyfriend?" he asks.

"High school best friend," I say.

"You're a lesbian?" He looks at me and I can tell he'd be happier if I said yes.

"Guy best friend," I say, and I can't help but laugh a little.

"Right," he says. "The one who noticed you even when you were a wallflower."

"Yeah," I say, looking down at my hands again and appreciating once more how genuine Oliver is.

"I should go," he says, standing up. I don't stop him. When he gets to the door, he turns around. "So . . . see you in Soc?"

"Okay," I say, waving. Is it dorky to wave at this moment? Probably.

When the door closes, I feel sort of sad, but also good. Simple and cheesy as it sounds, it's totally freeing to be honest.

nineteen

I'm avoiding my cell phone because Angela keeps calling. I have no idea why. She left me, and that puts me in the clear as far as returning messages are concerned, I think. I talked to my parents about it, and they are all for me signing with another agency if I want to keep modeling, but I'm not sure that's what I want. It wasn't totally Angela's fault that I wanted to quit—it was more than that. I promised Mom I'd think about it after this semester's over, but for now, I have to focus on school.

I need to play academic catch-up. In college, they let you be pretty independent—no homework every day, no weekly tests or anything like high school—but then they crack down and make *sure* you've been doing that independent-style work by giving you a monster-ass midterm or a big paper. I'm suddenly realizing that I'm not totally cruising here.

Jess, Fan, Kurt, and I have built in study breaks—one fifteen-minute break every two hours—where we get to snack on chips, drink soda, and talk competitively about our workloads to see who is the most stressed. Then we return to our individual study stations, a.k.a. our rooms.

It's kind of a bonding time for the whole campus, I've noticed. Everyone's walking around with these tortured grimaces on, doling out sympathy, but we're all in the same boat so it's a shared experience, which somehow makes it okay. It also has been easy to avoid Oliver, since no one's doing anything social and parties are rare this week before break.

Still, when I get back from the English department after turning in my analysis of symbolism in Faulkner's *As I Lay Dying*, I feel a huge weight off my shoulders. Until I see Kurt standing in our common room with his suitcase and helping Jess zip her duffel bag around a big beach towel.

"Don't worry, pumpkin," says Kurt, noticing my sad face. "We'll think of you every time we down an umbrella drink."

"I can't believe I have to work during spring break," I say. I've taken the last two Fridays off from my internship so I could study, but I promised Marilyn Flynn I'd be there every day these two weeks. The truth is that I'm trying to avoid a certain true love of mine—and his curly-haired girlfriend. The more I get to know Chloe, the more real a person she becomes and the less easy it is to write her off. I mean, yes, her laugh is annoying. But that's not a reason to hate someone.

"Have you talked to Roger yet?" asks Fan, coming out of her room with a bright orange bag rolling behind her.

Kurt gives her a big "no" head shake to get her to stop asking questions about Roger, but it's not very subtle.

"It's okay," I say. "No, I haven't talked to him at all." Not since the night at Marquee. No IMs even. I know for a fact that he's been online a lot—I've seen his Facebook updates—but I'm trying (somewhat unsuccessfully) not to care that he hasn't reached out.

"It'll be fine," says Fan. She has a who-gives attitude, but it's laced with an it-all-works-out-in-the-end positivity that makes it not harsh, which is nice. She's more carefree than uncaring.

"Hugs!" shouts Kurt, and we all put our arms around each other in the middle of the common room. "See you after break!"

As they grab their bags and leave, it seems weird to me that I just met these people a couple of months ago, but I'm already going to miss them while they're away for just two weeks. The hall gets really quiet as I pack up my clothes for the train ride into the city. I have to bring my best stuff since I'll be working for ten days, so I'm trying to fit a lot into my garment bag—DVF wrap dress, Alice Temperley scarf, Proenza Schouler blouse—things that I think adult types will appreciate.

On the train I take up a whole row of seats, but it doesn't really matter because it's not crowded. I hang onto Funny Monkey and let my iPod cycle through love songs. I definitely get some sick pleasure out of torturing myself with music. I listen to U2's "All I Want Is You" over and over because it makes me think of Roger. And because I enjoy self-inflicted angst.

I haul my crap through Grand Central and onto the subway bound for Brooklyn. When I get to Rita's house I ring the bell, but there's no answer so I use the "hidden" key. I look out the kitchen window and see that she's in the garden throwing a pot or something, even though the temperature is in the fifties and it's gray outside. I throw my things down in the Raggedy Ann room and then pull on an extra sweater so I can go sit with her. I'm feeling lonely.

"Hey, kiddo," says Rita when I push open the back door. "Your mom called."

"Oh yeah?" I say.

"Yeah, she was just checking in," says Rita.

"I've been crazy with midterms," I say. "I haven't really been good at returning calls."

"So I hear," says Rita. "It's not just your mom. I've fielded some other calls too."

"From who?" I ask, feeling my pulse quicken as I hope she'll say Roger.

"Angela," says Rita.

I roll my eyes. Of course it would make no sense for Roger to call here to find me. Angela, however, always has an angle.

"Why is she calling *you*?" I ask.

"She mentioned something about your contract, and a *Teen Fashionista* story you're doing," says Rita, being frustratingly vague. "I don't know, Violet. She says you haven't answered her calls. Why don't you call her back?"

"She dropped me!" I say. "She point-blank fired me. I don't understand why we need to talk."

"It's not that simple, honey," says Rita. "As long as there are designers and editors who still know your name, Angela will somehow want a piece of it."

I pick at the warped wood on Rita's picnic table, pulling off a sliver and turning it around over my fingers. *When will I be able to leave Angela behind?*

I spend the weekend being really low-key with Rita, and she doesn't mention Angela again. She knows I need some downtime after my exams, and that thinking about work stuff just stresses me out.

On Monday morning, though, I'm headed into *Teen Fashionista* in a Diane von Furstenburg wrap dress that kind of makes me feel like I'm thirty, but also looks professional, I decide. Even though these two weeks are still intern duty, it seems more serious since I'll be going in every day.

When I get to the office, I see that Alexia has taken over my cube in the two Fridays that I've been out. There's a used Jamba Juice cup by the phone, and her login screen is up. I roll my eyes, but realize that I can't say anything. I restart the computer and throw away her nasty cup.

Then I hear Chloe calling my name. "Violet? Are you here?"

I haven't seen her since the night Roger and I skipped out on everyone to hang out alone, but she's acting like her singsong, cheerful self. I'm sure Roger wouldn't tell her what I said to him—would he?

"Hi, Chloe," I say, smiling.

"Marilyn wants to see you," she says. "There's someone in her office, too. Your agent."

"Angela?" I ask, my eyes getting wide.

"Right," says Chloe as she turns to walk back to her desk.

My palms start to sweat as I head down the hallway toward Marilyn's corner office. *Why is Angela here?*

Marilyn Flynn's assistant, Susannah, sees me coming down the hall and waves me into Marilyn's office. I glance at the clock on her desk. *Am I late?* But I'm not—it's nine fifty-three a.m. and I'm officially supposed to be here at ten.

"Vibrant Violet!" I hear, as I enter Marilyn Flynn's office. There, on the black-and-white mod couch, is Angela. She's wearing four-inch Jimmy Choos and has a Birkin bag by her feet that I know for a fact has a yearlong waiting list.

I smile nervously at Marilyn Flynn, then at my ex-agent.

"Sit, sit," says Marilyn Flynn. "Angela was just telling me about all the calls she gets about you. I'm going to have Chloe interview her to round out our piece—it's still being edited."

They're going to interview Angela *for the story about how I'm a real girl with real problems who just happens to be a model?* "Oh, okay," I say. I start to smile and then I realize that I'm doing it again—I'm being completely passive about something I object to.

"So like I was saying," starts Angela. "Violet has been a wonder—"

"Wait," I interrupt. "Can I ask a question?"

"Of course, darling," says Angela, sounding sweeter than I've ever heard her.

"Didn't you fire me?" I ask. And even though my instinct is to look down at the white carpet, I will myself to meet her stare, and I think I see a flicker of fear.

"Oh, you mean that little spat we got into?" says Angela, putting on a stiff smile. She turns to Marilyn Flynn. "That was nothing! A teenager's overly dramatic mind at work . . ."

But I'm not planning on letting her get away with this. "No," I say. "I think you fired me. I'm pretty sure your exact words were 'You're no longer a Tryst girl.'"

"What's this all about?" asks Marilyn Flynn, looking at me with sympathy. Then she turns to Angela. "Angela, you told me there had been a reconciliation. Are you Violet's agent or aren't you?"

"She's still under contract," says Angela, blinking nervously. I don't think I've ever seen her off balance before. "And as long as people are asking for her at go-sees, she is obligated to—"

"I don't think she's obligated to do much of anything for you," says Marilyn Flynn, standing up and motioning through the door for her assistant. "Susannah, please show Ms. Blythe to the elevators."

"Valuable Violet," says Angela, appealing to me. "You know you've always been one of Tryst's shining stars."

"I haven't felt that way in a long time," I say to her. And I'm not being mean, or spiteful, or even especially angry. I'm just telling her the truth.

Angela meets my eyes and nods. Then she gathers up her $4,000 bag, flashes a smile at Marilyn Flynn, and follows Susannah down the hall. The woman knows how to make a dignified exit, even under fire.

After talking to Marilyn Flynn about how the real story is that I'm *not* going back to modeling, at least not in any serious way, she gives me a motherly pat on the back and says, "Let's leave Angela Blythe out of the story, then." She turns around and sits down at her desk, so I assume that's my cue to leave. Marilyn Flynn's been really nice to me, but I'm not about to hang out in her office and discuss my problems.

When I get back to my cube, I hear my cell phone message indicator beep, so I dial star-eighty-six to check it.

Veronica's voice says, "Hey, it's me. Just wanted to tell you that Mirabella is flying into New York this weekend, and she wants us both to be at an event. She specifically requested you, Violet. I hope you can make it."

I hang up the phone. That must be why Angela was in such a hurry to get me back—Mirabella is asking for me.

I stare at my computer screen for a while, trying to get a start on printing out mailing labels for invites to a *Teen Fashionista* party next week. But I realize that I won't be able to concentrate until I talk to Veronica, so I call her back.

"Hey," I say when she picks up.

"Hey!" She sounds excited to hear from me.

"Sorry I've been out of touch," I say. "Midterms."

"Right, right," she says. "College-speak. I get it."

"Listen—about that night at Marquee—" I start.

"Oh, don't worry," she says. "I know what happened. You and Roger wanted alone time. Sam and I handled it. Chloe was sloshed!"

"It wasn't quite like that," I say. "It was more like an error in judgment on my part."

"What do you mean?" asks Veronica.

But I don't feel like going into it, so I just say, "Nothing. What's going on with the Mirabella event?"

"Oh—it's this *huge* deal," she says, perking up. "She's having this party at the Soho Grand and *everyone* is going to be there. We need you, too. I know you're doing your college thing, but it would really help the campaign. Can you just make this one appearance? For me?"

It's the last two words that get me. I don't care about helping Mirabella's misguided "healthy body messages from high fashion models" campaign—I'd much rather do a sincere, love-yourself Girl Scouts ad. But if Veronica needs me . . .

"Okay," I say. "I'll come."

"Yes!" screams Veronica. "I'm *so* glad you're back, and we can—"

"I'm not back," I say, interrupting.

"Well, I just mean back for the party and maybe ready to get into the spotlight again and do some work together," says Veronica. "I mean, in the summer after you finish the semester at Vassar. You are coming back . . . aren't you, V?"

"No," I say. "I'm not." I'm surprised at how calm and resolute my voice sounds. Something about the fact that Marilyn Flynn still wants to do a story about me—even when she knows I'm getting out of the modeling world—has given me stronger resolve.

There's a pause, and I'm worried that Veronica is going to hate me and hang up or something, but then she says, "Oh, okay! We can talk about it Saturday." She sounds fake cheerful, like she doesn't believe—or doesn't want to believe—I'd really give up modeling. What she doesn't realize is that I already have.

On Saturday night at the Soho Grand, the garden is lit up with statues wearing Mirabella Prince designs. There are tiny appetizers, trays of champagne and mojitos, and lots of wild fashion people with larger-than-life personalities. I can hardly hear myself think through the exaggerated compliments everyone is screaming at each other. I'm wearing a silk gunmetal dress with lots of complicated layers. It's by FORM, and the designer—Jerry Tam—sent it to me last year after I did a show with him. I see him by the DJ booth and give him a quick cheek-kiss. He's always been great to me. Then I feel a tug on my arm and Veronica is leading me back to the front entrance—and the paparazzi.

When Veronica and I finally get off the red carpet, my eyes are burning from the flashbulbs and I'm wondering which blog will be the first to post a comment about how I'm no longer "pin thin." The freeing part is that I don't even care that much—it'll actually be fun to laugh with Kurt about it.

"Evil eye to your right," whispers Veronica as we move through the crowd upstairs to a booth that's been saved for us. I look over quickly and see Angela glaring at me. I smile and wave, feeling bolder than usual. I am *so over* this world.

When we sit down, I realize that our corner booth isn't very private. There's a light shining on us, and I see people pointing as the waiter brings a bottle of champagne to the table.

"Not exactly cozy," I say to Veronica as she flashes a smile to the onlookers.

"We're working tonight," says Veronica, through her smile. It doesn't look forced, though. It's actually like Veronica *loves* this moment.

"You're really having fun, aren't you?" I ask, full of wonder at the idea of enjoying a thousand people staring and flashbulbs going off and older women whispering about your hair and eye makeup and clothes and weight. I mean, when I first started modeling I got a thrill out of what I thought was the excitement and the adoration of people who saw me on the runway or in a magazine. But what I realized was that they were all talking behind my back, judging me on what I looked like rather than who I am, making up rumors and generally being vicious and awful when I'd done nothing to them. The only part I still really care about are the girls who are my fans, like the ones at the school in Brooklyn.

"I didn't clean up and land a new campaign so I could fade into obscurity," says Veronica. And that's the difference between us. To me, obscurity sounds absolutely fabulous right about now.

But I put on a smile—for Veronica—and when Mirabella comes over to sit with us and flashbulbs rain down once again, I even go in for a double air-kiss.

"Violet!" trills Mirabella. "You've been hiding from me!" She leans back in the booth to take in my dress, which is gorgeously forgiving with flowing fabrics and a billowing skirt. Then she pinches my arm. *She actually pinches my arm!*

"I don't mind that you've gained some weight," she says. "The campaign is done. Your photograph is beautiful."

I look over at Veronica, who's biting her lip and staring at me sympathetically. Then I smile at Mirabella. "Thank you," I say. "I'm glad it's over, too."

After another half hour of annoying talk about her new line and Veronica's summer plans ("work, work, work!") I'm itching to leave.

I haven't said a word in twenty minutes besides, "Oh," and "That's nice." B-O-R-I-N-G.

"Bathroom, Veronica?" I ask, giving her get-me-out-of-here eyes.

When we reach the restroom's entrance, I finally let out my breath. "I think I'm gonna go," I say to Veronica.

"What?!" she snaps, her eyes turning into slits. "You can't leave me now!"

"I'm not even *talking*," I say.

"But you're there," she says. "It's important, V. To me."

"*Why?*" I ask, truly curious. "I'm tired and bored and sick of people looking at me."

"They're all just admiring your beauty," says Veronica, smiling, trying to charm her way into getting me to stay.

"Please!" I say. "They're all gossiping about how I gained ten pounds."

"Don't listen to them," says Veronica. "You still look thin. And you'll lose that weight. It's just from college and having a different diet."

"Veronica, that is *so* not the point," I say, exasperated. "I don't *want* to lose the weight. I think I look *better* with ten pounds on me!"

"You look great, Violet," she says, looking in the mirror to reapply her mascara. "But if we want to land a major campaign, we have to be in high-fashion shape."

"Which basically means high-eating-disorderville?" I ask sarcastically.

"*Why* are you being so difficult?!" screams Veronica.

"*Why* can't you understand that I'm out?! I quit! I'm done!" I shout back. "I only came here tonight as a favor to you!"

Veronica looks at me like I slapped her. At first, I think she might lunge at me or say something crazy-mean like she used to when we lived together. But what she does surprises me. She goes over to one of the plush red stools in the corner, sits down, and starts to cry.

I squat next to her and put my hand on her bony back. I can see her spine through the thin gold sheath she's wearing.

"I need you," she says, through tears. "My career is nothing without you."

"What are you talking about?" I ask, my eyes widening. "You're Veronica Trask—everyone wants you!"

"They don't," she says. "Wherever I am, they always ask for you. 'Where's Violet?' 'Where's your better half, Double V?' It's like I'm living in your shadow."

"I don't even have a shadow anymore," I say. "And they're just saying that because they liked our Double V gimmick! They'll get over it."

"I'm not sure I can book another big job without you, V," says Veronica.

"Of course you can," I say. "You're an amazing model, and you really love what you do. For me, it's different. After the excitement wore off, I felt like I was losing a part of myself by modeling. For you, it makes you more of who you are."

I realize that I'm sounding like a self-help guru, but I think I'm speaking some truths here because Veronica starts crying even harder.

"I'm sorry," she says, sniffling as I hand her a tissue.

"It's okay," I say.

"No, it's not," she says. "I've been trying to use you, and you've been my only true friend this whole year."

"Use me?" I ask, stiffening a little.

"I wormed my way into the Mirabella campaign when it was sup- posed to be all yours, I've told Angela that you didn't want to do any press and I never called you to tell you about the events or parties, I even gave Chloe a mean quote for the *Teen Fashionista* story!" Veronica leans over into my lap and clings to my waist. "I'm so sorry!" she cries.

I'm not sure how to respond. On the one hand, the things she did were malicious and deceptive. But on the other hand, I'm *glad* she joined the Mirabella campaign and *grateful* that she did all the schmoozing at events. One thing she mentioned does bother me, though.

"What did you say to Chloe?" I ask.

"I told her you were never really a model," says Veronica, her voice muffled because her head's still in my lap. "I told her you were always more of a girl from North Carolina who didn't belong in the modeling world."

I think about what Veronica said for a moment. To her, that would be one of the most backhanded, evil things to say about someone. But to me, it actually sounds kind of like the truth.

I pat Veronica's shoulder and nudge her to sit up. She looks at me, scared of my reaction.

"Hey," I say, making sure she's looking in my eyes. "We're real friends. Not the type of friends who do stuff behind each other's backs, and not the type of friends who lie to each other."

"I know," she says, her face dropping as another tear falls. "I *want* to be that type of friend." Then she gulps in some air and starts really crying again. "I just keep screwing it all up and doing the wrong thing. Maybe I'm a bad person who can't—"

"Shhh," I say, stopping her trainwreck rant. "Veronica, you're not a bad person. You're just messy."

She looks up again, and I smile at her. "Who wouldn't be?" I continue. "Fashion is effed up."

"I'm so sorry, Violet." Veronica grabs a tissue for her tears. "I'm hideously insecure lately. It doesn't wear well, I know."

"It's okay," I say. "You are still spellbindingly hot."

"*Spellbindingly?*" I see her mouth turn up slightly.

"I forgive you on one condition," I say.

"What?" asks Veronica, blowing her nose.

"Tell me what mascara you're wearing," I say. "All that crying and not a single streak."

Veronica laughs and we share a long hug. Not a fashion world hug where you stand back to avoid wrinkling, but a real friend hug. Then she takes my hand as we walk out of the bathroom together. She lets go and strides back to the VIP table while I put my head down to avoid the cameras and find a side exit onto the street.

twenty

I take a cab to Brooklyn and almost fall asleep in the backseat. I can barely keep my eyes open, which is why, when I see a figure sitting on Rita's stoop, I'm sure that I'm hallucinating.

"Roger?" I whisper as I approach the stoop. Hopefully it's not a scary man in a black hoodie who just *looks* like Roger. That would suck.

He doesn't respond, but when I get closer, Roger stands up and smiles. "I was waiting," he says.

"Well, you didn't have to sit outside," I say, starting a nervous, uncontrollable babble. "I mean, Rita knows you and she would have totally let you in if you'd just rung the buzzer."

Roger just stares at me with a silly smile.

Silence is weird. Must. Keep. Talking. "It may be spring break, but it's still cold at night so you should really—"

Roger puts his hand up to make me be quiet. And then he

reaches for me and pulls me close. I completely forget to breathe when he kisses me. And then I lose all sense of anything except his lips, and his hands on my face.

We part after what seems like a split second that lasted hours. Roger looks at me intently, like he wants me to know that he meant that kiss. That we can't play it off like we did in Barcelona. That this is really happening.

When I take his hand and lead him inside and downstairs to the Raggedy Ann room where I've been guest-sleeping since I was a little girl, I know what I'm doing. And I feel completely ready for it—whatever *it* is.

When we get to the guest bedroom, Roger reaches for me as soon as I shut the door. My brain is Jell-O but somehow my lips are doing just what they're supposed to, and I start walking backward toward the bed, tugging at Roger's shirt.

He takes off his sweater and I pull him down onto the soft quilt. I move backward until Roger is lying on top of me, kissing me and pushing up the skirt of my dress. I'm going to let this happen. I'm not afraid or nervous or even embarrassed—I just feel like I need this, like I've waited for it.

My heart is pounding as Roger sits up and slips my dress over my head. He unhooks my bra with one hand, which surprises me a little. *I thought he'd be more awkward.*

He tugs off his own jeans and lies back down next to me. We're both in our underwear. I breathe in deeply and close my eyes. This is it. This is the real thing. I'm going to do this.

Suddenly, I hear Roger chuckle. I open my eyes. He's smirking and holding up my stuffed animal.

"Funny Monkey made it to New York?" He's mocking me.

"I couldn't leave him behind!" I smile.

Roger leans in to kiss me again, but now that we're pausing, I have to ask him something.

"When did you break up with Chloe?" I look him in the eye, smiling, so happy that we finally got the timing right, that we can be together.

But he's not meeting my gaze. He's looking down at the quilt and fingering a loose red thread.

"Roger?" I ask.

"I didn't," says Roger.

My heart starts pounding, but not in the way it was a few seconds ago. This pounding is angry, and I squint my eyes to force back the tears that are about to come hard and fast.

"What?" I ask. "What do you mean?"

"It's complicated, Violet," he says.

"No, it's not!" I shout, pushing him off me and standing to grab my bra. I reach for his sweater and throw it at him. He's sits up, looking defeated.

"Get out," I say, trying to control my volume so Rita won't hear. I pick up my dress to cover myself. I suddenly feel so uncomfortable, so exposed.

"Just let me expl—" he starts, but his phone interrupts.

The Temptations blast from his pocket. *Chloe.*

"'My Girl.' Are you fucking kidding me?" I say, almost to myself.

He pulls on his jeans and looks down at the ground while he stuffs his hands into his pocket and silences the phone. I'm sure he'll call her back as soon as he's out of here. He gets dressed quickly and when he tries to talk again, I give him a look that says *I don't want to hear it.*

I show him to the basement-floor door. It's below the stoop and

Rita rarely uses it, so I have to grab a key hanging on the wall to un-lock it from the inside.

I'm in a daze. I think Roger says *good-bye* or *see you later* or some-thing equally lame and insufficient, given the situation, and then I relock the door and go into the bathroom.

I turn on the faucet and let the water run on full blast while I sit on the toilet seat and stare at the tiles. I don't know what to think. *Am I some sort of other woman? A cheap spring break hookup?*

And then I start crying. The kind of crying where you can't really make any noise and you have to take in big gulps of air. *What just happened?*

twenty-one

When I go to work on Monday, I'm still in a fog. As soon as I sit down at my desk, I hear a gaggle of giggles coming down the hall. I peek around the corner of my cube and see four editors gathered around Chloe, whose smile is so big she looks like Julia Roberts on happy juice.

I quickly pull my head back into my cube and stare at the computer screen as I sit perfectly still so I can hear every word they say.

"Gramercy Tavern is a little cliché, but still sweet," I hear Valentina the beauty editor say.

"Oooh, it's so adorable," says Fiona, a fashion assistant. "Your college boy making upscale dinner reservations. What's the occasion?"

"I don't know," says Chloe. "He wanted to go out yesterday but I was super-busy, so he insisted he *had* to see me tonight. I think he might ask if I want to get an apartment with him next year!"

She says this last part with such annoying glee that I want to take out her vocal cords with the staple remover on my desk.

I stand up stiffly and hurry past them toward the handicapped bathroom—the one where you can lock yourself in and be alone without having to check under the stalls. I shove a wad of paper towels in my mouth and bite down hard as I start to cry. I know that my screams will be too loud otherwise.

He loves her. *He wants to move in with her. He wants to live with a honk-snort-laughing, overly jovial, curly-haired, five-foot-nothing pixie girl.*

For five minutes, I just feel bad. I feel sorry for myself, I feel a huge sense of loss, I make big ugly faces in the mirror as my mouth distorts and the tears burst out. And then I let myself feel the betrayal.

Roger isn't supposed to be deceptive like this—not with me. What we had, our friendship, was like this perfect, pure thing. In my heart, I know that if we hadn't stopped the other night, I would have slept with him. And it would have been a lie. He would have let that happen.

Suddenly, I get angry. *Fuck him*, I think, using the coarse paper towels to dry my face. I pinch my cheeks to renew the color that was drained from them by the sound of Chloe's chipper chirping. I stare in the mirror, determined to be strong, to hold my head up and not let this tragedy of epic proportions beat me. I start remembering inspirational scenes from my favorite always-on-TBS movies, like how Renée Zellweger regains her dignity after getting jerked around by Hugh Grant in *Bridget Jones*, how Julia Stiles learns to dance again after her mom dies in *Save the Last Dance*, how Shane West goes on to become a better person after he loses Mandy Moore in *A Walk to Remember*. Okay, so no one died here, but to me it feels like that. It feels like my heart has been torn out of my chest like in some bloody horror movie.

I wish I lived in a movie and not real life. I want an inspirational music makeover scene where my life is cleaned up and I end up looking fabulous and freshly shampooed in less than the length of Natasha Bedingfield's "Unwritten." I will get over Roger, I will not let this change who I am, I will love again! I may even write a Top 40 hit with all this material.

And even as I'm giving myself this ultra-inspiring mental pep talk and drying off my face, there's a little voice in my head that's still asking, *"How could he do this to me?"*

I tell Chloe I'm not feeling well, and she says I can leave early. I've already sent out invitations for the magazine's big party, so I really have nothing to do anyway. When the F train goes aboveground as I ride back to Rita's house, I see that I have a voice mail.

"Violet," says his voice. "Please talk to me."

How can Roger call me right now? I delete the message and his number from my cell phone, although that's more of a meaningless gesture—I've had it memorized since ninth grade.

As soon as I get off the subway and start walking to Rita's, the phone rings again—919. Roger. No way. Not answering. It keeps ringing though. He's calling over and over. Finally, he leaves a message. And I know if I were really bad-ass I'd just delete it without listening, but I've never been one of those girls who can do that—I'm too curious.

"Violet, I know you're avoiding me," he says. "Please call."

I don't.

For one, that was a really boring message. If he had something good to say, he should make his case over voice mail because I'm not risking picking up the phone to get lied to all over again.

I'm relieved that Rita isn't home when I get to her house, and I sit down at the well-worn kitchen table to write Roger a good-bye letter. I grab a yellow legal pad—he doesn't deserve nice stationery.

I try a few different drafts. One where I'm pouring my heart out, one that asks him *whywhywhy?*, one that is designed to hurt him by listing a few childhood memories that I will carry with me even though we're no longer friends. I settle on a scrawled message just says, "Leave me alone. Violet Greenfield." I feel like using my last name creates more distance between us, and that will sting.

As I rifle through Rita's desk drawers looking for a stamp, my phone rings again. It's 212—I hope it's not Chloe.

"Violet." It's Roger. Dorm phone. He's always been tricky.

"I don't want to talk to you." I can feel my heart in my throat.

"It's not what you think—" he says.

"Are you still with Chloe?" I ask.

"Yes, but—"

I hang up and turn off my phone. What more do I need to know?

Then Rita's landline starts going off, so I run around the house turning all the ringers to silent. I don't want her to talk to Roger either. He's officially cut off from my whole family.

I tear up the messy message I wrote to him—he doesn't even deserve that.

I get online and erase him as a friend from MySpace and Facebook. I block him, too, so he can't bug me. Then I go to flip.com. Girls need to know about him.

It takes me about two hours to create a virtual scrapbook of angst about Roger. I set it to Pink's "Who Knew," and I upload pictures of abstract things like thunderstorms and wilted flowers and jerky Hollywood guys like Chuck from *Gossip Girl* to express my heartache. Then I start in on the "anger" pages, where I'm uploading actual photos of Roger and drawing devil horns on him and blacking out his teeth. I'm not sure I'm going to publicly post this thing, but it's cathartic.

Still, I don't know how I'm ever going to get over this betrayal. It's completely weird how your heart can physically hurt. Like, I can feel this actual pain in my chest right now, and I'm not just imagining it. It aches, like if someone hit me really hard on my left boob, or like I broke something there.

The next morning, I call in sick to work. I can't face Chloe or hear about her and Roger's romantic dinner. I briefly wonder if I should tell her what happened, but that seems so soap-opera-y. Mostly I just want to forget it all, so I spend the day in bed. Rita works from home, but she accepts that I'm feeling sick so she leaves me alone all day.

A little after four p.m., while I'm watching *Oprah* on the tiny TV downstairs, I hear someone tapping on the basement windows. I look through the dusty glass and past the iron bars to see Roger's pensive face.

I shake my head no. I don't want Rita to know he's here, and I need him to go away. When he doesn't, I grab the comforter off my bed and cover the window with it so I can't see him anymore. He's always been good at picking up on social cues, but today is an exception.

Two minutes later, Aunt Rita's involved.

"Violet!" she shouts down the stairs. "Roger's here!"

I can't believe he has this much nerve. I feel like a trapped animal down here. He's at the door, the backyard is sealed in, and I don't want Rita to figure out there's anything wrong. . . .

I decide to go into "who cares" mode. I don't brush my hair or even change out of my sweatpants as I head upstairs to face Roger. I smile for Aunt Rita, and then I usher him out onto the front porch. I do not want him inside the house.

When Rita closes the door, I sit down on the stoop and stare at the cracks in the sidewalk below us. Roger sits on the stair below me, but not too close. At least he's reading *some* cues.

"I broke up with Chloe last night," Roger says.

The hair on my arm stands up, but I keep my eyes focused on the pavement.

"Violet, did you hear me?" he asks when I don't respond.

"I heard you," I say quietly.

"It's always been you," he says, like we're on some TV show and he can say a line like that and I'll turn to him and everything will be okay. But this isn't a stupid TV show. And he just can't do this to me—or Chloe.

"What you did was wrong," I say.

"I never told you that Chloe and I were broken up," he says.

"You knew what I would assume!" I shout, looking up into his eyes for the first time. And they look so pained that I want to tell him it's all okay, and that we're still best friends and maybe more. But I can't.

"Come on, Violet, it was *right*. I know you felt that too." I can feel Roger's eyes.

"You took something from me," I say, leveling my tone and returning my gaze to the pavement as I remember that I was trying to stay in "who cares" mode. I do *not* want to get emotional.

"We barely got to second base!" he says.

"I'm not talking about my virginity," I say, because I'm not. I've never thought in terms of my special treasure like those girls who wear the True Love Waits rings—it's just not my take on sex. This is bigger than that.

"Then what are you talking about?" Roger asks.

"You took away my unconditional trust in *us*," I say. "I shouldn't have to explain that to you. It was a betrayal of our friendship. Not to mention a shitty thing to do to your girlfriend, cheater."

Roger's head drops down and he puts his hands over his eyes like he's going to cry. Part of me wants to reach out to him, but more of me is raging mad. Our first real passionate moment was Roger cheating on his girlfriend! *Doesn't he see how he's ruined everything? That what we had was supposed to be untouchable and perfect?* He made things shameful.

"You're my best friend, Violet," Roger says, finally. His voice is cracking a little bit. "I've been in love with you since we were in first grade. I was waiting for you to—"

He pauses and looks up at me. His blue eyes are soft and sad.

"Sometimes," he says, "when I was with Chloe, it felt like I was cheating on *you*."

"That is really messed up, Roger," I say. "That isn't how things are supposed to be." I think about how I let Oliver down early, because I knew he wasn't the one I wanted. It's not like I see myself as all high and mighty for doing the right thing, but I just can't listen to Roger try to justify his relationship with Chloe and hooking up with me while he was still with her.

"I think you should go," I say to him.

"But I always thought when the timing was right, when you saw me the way I've seen you all this time, that things would be okay," says Roger. "That they'd just work out and we'd be together."

"You were wrong," I say, crossing my arms across my chest and walking back into Rita's house. I double-bolt the door when I get inside. Just before I collapse to the floor and cry.

twenty-two

After my big meltdown in the entryway, I had to tell Rita something. I said that Roger and I had a fight and we're no longer friends. She asked a few questions but didn't pry much, which I really appreciate. Then she said, "Time fixes things," and made me a tuna melt. I didn't bother telling her that years and years will not fix *this*.

When I get Julie on the phone that night, I start crying again. She tries to comfort me, but I know she's in a weird position since Roger is her best friend too. Nothing is making this better.

I call in sick for the rest of the week—how could I go in to the office and see Chloe?—but I have to pick up some of my things on Friday before I head back up to school.

I get to the Bruton building a little before nine a.m. so I can avoid seeing anyone, but while I'm grabbing the Sociology book I was supposed to be reading all week, I hear a rustling behind me.

"Hi, Violet," says Chloe.

I turn, feeling my face flush and my chin start to tremble at the sight of her.

She looks awful. Sad and tired and beaten down. I wonder if I did this to her. In a sort of indirect way, but still. I'm not good with guilt.

"Hi, Chloe," I manage. "You're here early."

"I have work to catch up on," she says. "I took a couple of days off—heartache leave."

I wince.

"Are you feeling okay?" she asks.

"Oh, yeah," I say, remembering that I'm supposed to be on the brink of death with a mondo cold. I do one of those faint coughs that everyone tries when they're faking it. So lame. "I think I'm almost over the bug I had. I'm sorry about work this week."

"It's okay," she says. "I didn't have the best week either, as I'm sure you heard."

I search her eyes for any sign that she knows about me and Roger. I have no idea if he told her what happened. But she's just staring blankly through me, no trace of malice in her face.

"I'm sorry about Roger," I say, feeling like a total douchebag jerk.

She waves her hand in front of her face like she doesn't even want to think about it. "Want to read your story?" she asks, holding out a folder that contains loose page proofs from the profile of me.

I'm half scared that she's got some version of the story where I'm portrayed as a boyfriend-stealing slut. But I see that the headline reads, "Isn't she lovely?" and the subhead reads, "Model Violet Greenfield makes us totally believe in inner beauty."

I glance through the pages and see that the story is incredibly flattering. It mentions my visit to meet high school girls, how I've managed to resist the stay-stick-thin pressures of the runway, and how I've kept up good friendships with people who aren't in the fashion world. There's a sidebar with quotes from real girls, one of the girls from Brooklyn even, talking about how the fashion industry makes them feel about their bodies.

In the top right corner of the spread, there's a photo of me and Roger that we took last year in Barcelona. It's a self-take, so we're at this weird angle and our heads are really big and filling the frame. I'm laughing in the shot because it's like the fifth time we tried to get the picture right. The caption reads, "Traveling in Barcelona with her BFF Roger Stern."

I guess Chloe sees me staring at it, because she says, "He gave me that picture to use before—" And then she starts to cry.

I find myself hugging her and patting her back as she sobs on my shoulder. I stare, wide-eyed, at the cube across from mine, which is decorated with that "Hang in There" poster where the cat is dangling on a laundry line or something. I think the features editor did that to be ironic. This moment is bizarre. I'm pretty sure Chloe doesn't know anything, but that doesn't help my guilt much.

When she calms down a bit, she apologizes and reaches for a tissue on my desk. "I really cared about him, you know?" she says.

I nod, but I don't speak. I really don't want to encourage a drama session where she confides in me.

"I mean, I don't know if you've ever had a long-term relationship like mine and Roger's," she says.

"Not really," I say, thinking that less than a year isn't exactly golden anniversary time. But that's a bitchy thought, so I try to push it away. Why am I a jerk?

"It's just hard," she says, taking a deep breath through her nose and breathing out through her mouth. That's what Julie's life coach says to do when you're stressed. I wonder if Chloe has a life coach.

I wonder if she's deeper than I thought. "I'll be okay, though," she continues, and she grabs my hand and squeezes it. "Thanks, Violet."

Triple shame. I grab my things and wave. "See you next Friday," I say.

"Feel better," says Chloe.

I am such an asshole.

As I'm leaving the Bruton building, my phone rings.

"Hey, Veronica," I say, starting to walk east toward Grand Central.

"V, there's a great party this weekend!" She launches into her you-have-to-be-there-because-everyone-is-going talk. Shouldn't she know this won't work on me?

"Can't make it," I say. "I've had a bad week. Something happened with Roger."

"What?" asks Veronica.

"The worst," I say, almost starting to cry but holding it in by biting my lip really hard.

"Where are you?" asks Veronica.

"Walking to Grand Central," I say. "I'm going back to campus."

"I'm coming," says Veronica. "I just have to finish this shoot I'm on, but I'll see you tonight."

"You don't have to—" I start.

"No argument!" shouts Veronica. "I'll be there by eight." She hangs up before I can raise another protest.

On the train to Poughkeepsie, I get out my calendar and flip to all those "notes" pages in the back. I never use these pages for anything other than the random address I think I'll forget, or a quick scrawl to get a pen's ink flowing. But right now I feel like making a list to organize my (somewhat self-hating) thoughts. Call it an emotional get-through-it list, or use the title I write down at the top, "Things That Are Wrong with My Life" (subtitle: "Why I'm Awful"):

1. I hooked up with a lying cheater.

2. My BFF Roger is a lying cheater.

3. I think Chloe is a perfectly nice girl, whom I have wronged.

4. I'm completely disconnected from the modeling world, and everyone has forgotten me. Do I want it that way? Then why do I feel empty now? (Oh yeah, could have something to do with #1.)

5. I've gained ten pounds.

6. I wish I didn't care that I've gained ten pounds. Like, at all. But I sort of do.

7. I am scared that, deep down, maybe I'm not a nice person.

I slam the planner shut and shove it into my bag as I slump down on the vinyl seat of the train and stare out the window at the Hudson River.

When I get back to my dorm, the halls are still quiet. I guess people won't return from break until Sunday. I curl up on my bed and fall asleep to the "In case of major heartache" playlist I made last year for my iPod—Otis Redding, Patsy Cline, and the Postal Service. I'm glad I had it ready.

I wake up to a soft tickle under my nose. I stretch my arms over my head and open my eyes.

"Kurt!" I shriek. He's waving a bejeweled pink thong over my face.

"Your present from the shore," he says, holding it up in the air.

"Classy," I say.

"Oh, please," he says, rolling his eyes. "Would you rather I got you a beach T-shirt? I thought this was more interesting."

I smile, so glad he's back. "Are Jess and Fan here?" I ask, pushing myself off the bed and realizing I've been asleep for like four hours.

"No," says Kurt. "They're at home for a few days. My dad still isn't the most comfortable with my, um, penchant for boys in tight tees, so I'd rather just be here."

I look at him for a second, wondering if he's about to get sad or open up to me, but then Kurt laughs and hops into the common area to grab me a beer.

I wonder why I never thought to ask him about his family, or how they feel about his being gay. I'm going to add "Completely self-involved" to my "Why I'm Awful" list as soon as I get the chance.

I walk out of my room and sit down on the couch with Kurt as he opens my beer for me. He knows I'm no good with pull tabs. I either break them off or drop them into the can, both of which make drinking really annoying and possibly dangerous.

"Thanks," I say. "So how was the beach?" I'm resolved to talk only about *his* spring break, to hear all about the adventures he and Fan and Jess had and not to say a word about my own issues.

"A blast," says Kurt. "Super-fun. A lot of drinking, a little hooking up—but nothing serious—and no, Jess did *not* find a guy. We have to break her out of her shy mold. And—"

"Maybe she's better off," I mumble under my breath.

"Huh?" asks Kurt.

"Nothing," I say, realizing that I'm *already* thinking about myself again.

"Did someone have some boy issues over break?" asks Kurt.

Well, he did ask . . .

Three hours later, I'm still on the couch with a box of tissues at my feet, only now Veronica has joined us and we're all eating pizza that we ordered from Napoli's. It's cheesy and greasy, and just what I want. Veronica has had two pieces so far, which is unheard of for her.

"Let me get this straight," says Veronica, picking at my crust remnants. "You and Roger—whom I know you've loved for, like, ever—*hook up,* then he breaks up with Chloe and then you tell him *good-bye.*"

"Right," I say.

"Explain to me again why?" she asks.

Kurt puts down his slice and raises his hand like we're in class. "I know, I know!" he shouts.

"Kurt." I call on him.

"Because Roger did things out of order. Breakups before hookups!" He smiles and gives me a high five.

"Okay," says Veronica. "But whatever. It's over now with Chloe. So why can't you be with him? You're a forgiver, Violet. You forgave me."

"Ooh, what'd you do to her?" asks Kurt, rubbing his hands together. He's been giddy since Veronica got here, though in the last hour he has stopped taking pictures of her every five minutes. Thank God.

"Nothing," says Veronica. "I mean, nothing unforgivable. Right, V?"

I smile at her. We've been joking around for a few minutes, after my two hours of sniffling and crying about Roger. I think I started laughing when I got buzzed from the beer I had. But now I feel the emotional roller coaster heading for another vertical drop.

"Uh-oh," says Kurt as I start to make the ugly cry face before any sound even comes out. "More tissues!"

Veronica bolts to the hall bathroom to steal another roll of thin, itchy toilet paper. When I scoff at it, Kurt says, "It's better than your sleeve." He has a point.

I blow my sore nose and swallow the lump in my throat. "I'm sorry, you guys," I say. "I am a total mess."

"Things are not so bad," says Kurt.

I eye him warily, because I know he's about to go into his "What are you grateful for?" speech. He did it when I got stressed out about midterms. It sort of worked, but it's also very cheesy.

"Let's make a grateful list," he says.

"Ooh, I saw this on *Oprah*. I'll get the markers!" says Veronica, clapping her hands together. "There are a bunch in Violet's room."

It's true. I love stationery stores and all colors of markers. But why is Veronica so all about this?

Kurt sprints to his room to grab *poster board*, of all things.

"I don't think I can fill that," I say, when he comes back with a huge blank canvas, his eyes shining. He is *way* too excited about hosting a self-help seminar right here in my common room.

"Silence, Negativa!" he commands, as he clears floor space for the poster board. Veronica plops down with a rainbow of markers and a sheet of stickers from my desk drawer. I still love stickers.

"How's your handwriting?" asks Kurt.

"Not good—you do it," Veronica says, handing off the red marker she's opened.

The two of them are like BFFs at summer camp, drawing a flower border around the edges before we begin. I'm slumped on the too-short futon with my legs thrown over the end and my eyes staring up at the ceiling. My posture is one way I'm trying to convey that I'm so not into this right now. No one notices.

"Okay, what's one thing you're thankful for?" asks Kurt after the flower border is completed.

"Um . . . pizza?" I say, knowing that's not what he wants to hear.

"Think bigger!" says Kurt.

"I know," I say. "The mini-fridge!"

He rolls his eyes and casts an exasperated glance at Veronica.

"I'll start for her," she says. "Violet is grateful that she gets to go to college on this gorgeous campus."

"Amen!" says Kurt, using a purple marker to write "VASSAR!" in the top corner of the poster. "And let's not forget that she's paying for tuition with money she got for standing around and looking pretty!"

"Hey!" Veronica and I say simultaneously.

Kurt giggles. "Okay, Tyras," he says. "I know there's more to modeling than that. I *guess*. You are both completely fierce. Can we move on?"

I smile and roll onto my side to face them.

Veronica turns out to be really good at thinking of things that are right with my life. Within twenty minutes, we've got the poster almost filled with: *Mom, Dad, Jake; international travel;* Teen Fashionista *internship; cool roommates; designer freebies; good genes; Aunt Rita; Louboutin heels* (Kurt thought they deserved a separate grateful space).

When Veronica says we should add Julie to the page, I cross my arms over my chest.

"Yup," I say, looking back at the ceiling. It's impossible for me to think of Julie without thinking of Julie and Roger. It's always been the three of us, so writing down "Julie" and leaving him out feels like amputating something. I'm like a war victim with a ghost limb. Okay, it's not that dramatic, but you get what I'm saying.

"And Roger?" asks Kurt.

I stare him down angrily. "Don't you dare add him to that poster!" I say.

"Listen, hon," says Kurt, putting on his from-New-York-but-moved-to-Florida grandmother voice. "I know he hurt you the other night."

"More than hurt!" I say. "Try total betrayal."

I see Kurt glance at Veronica, who shrugs.

"He didn't do things in order," says Veronica. "He got swept up in the emotion of seeing you. The guy's been in love with you for like fifteen years."

"Veronica's right," says Kurt. "Roger made a mistake. A big one, but still a mistake. It wasn't intentional hurt."

"I don't know," I say, trying to take in what they're saying.

"It isn't a deal breaker, V," says Veronica. "At least not for your friendship. I know we both know enough about what makes a real deal breaker."

She stares pointedly at me and I think back to my "relationships" with skeezy club promoter Peter Heller, who thought it was "tacky" when I visited Veronica in rehab, and Paulo Forte from São Paulo, Brazil, who totally cheated with another model. But the thing is, I hold Roger to a higher standard than other guys, because he's *Roger*.

"We were supposed to be perfect," I say quietly, staring at a beer stain on the futon pillow. "*Roger* is supposed to be perfect."

"But no one is," says Veronica. "You know that."

I look over at her and then at Kurt, who's raising his eyebrows in impatience.

"So can I write it or what?" he asks, green marker poised above the poster board.

"Okay," I say, thinking that maybe over the summer, Roger and I can talk. We can figure this out, right? Maybe things can heal slowly.

"Phew!" says Kurt, finishing up the final *r* in his fancy cursive rendition of Roger's name. "What else?"

"Violet is grateful that Kurt is such a good friend," says Veronica.

Kurt beams and writes his own name down on the paper. He outlines big bubble letters in orange and Veronica fills them in with a blue marker.

"And Violet is grateful to have you," says Kurt, pointing at Veronica.

Veronica looks up at me hesitantly—as if she's not sure I'll claim her. As if she's afraid I'll say she's not an important part of my life.

I smile at her. "Write it down, Double V!" I say, perking up a little as it dawns on me that she skipped the big party she'd been telling me about on the phone. She knew I needed her. And now she's making a silly poster with Kurt and acting like it's the greatest Friday night she's ever had.

"You're an amazing friend," I say to her. She scoots toward me on her knees and I lean over and we're giving each other this lying-down-seated-hug. Then we both start laughing and I roll off the couch entirely.

Kurt jumps up. "Gratitude poster works again!" he yells.

Just then my phone rings. I disentangle myself from Veronica and grab my bag. "It's Julie," I say, hoping she won't want to discuss the Roger thing right now. I've already walked her through it eight times . . . and she's caught in the middle but she swears on the Girl Code that she won't report anything I say back to him.

"Ooh, tell her about the poster!" says Kurt, filling in white space with pink glitter heart stickers. "Julie will love it."

"Hey," I say into the phone.

"Did you hear?" Julie asks.

And I'm almost afraid to say *What?* because I'm sure she's going to tell me that Roger and Chloe are back together. But I also *have* to know. "What?"

"Roger's going to L.A. this summer," she says. "He just called me and told me he got into some film study program at USC."

"Oh," I say, going numb.

"He didn't tell us he'd applied just in case he didn't get in," says Julie. "You know how he's like that."

"Yeah," I say, my mind starting to race. *No summer together. No time to fix anything.*

"Violet, he's completely miserable . . ." she says. "Are you forgiving him?"

"I don't know," I say. And it's the truth.

twenty-three

The next morning, Kurt and I drive Veronica to the train station.

"Best Friday night I've had in a long time," she says as she gives me a big hug. "Kurt, you are on my VIP list!"

He honks twice as she walks into the station.

"Happy about your all-access pass to any club in the city?" I ask him as we loop around and drive back to campus.

"I'm just happy to have a new friend," he says.

I snicker.

"Okay, yeah, also the cachet of knowing Veronica Trask is nice," Kurt admits. "But she's a good friend too!"

"Yeah, she's learning." I smile to myself.

When we get back to the dorm, I go downstairs to check my mail buildup. After two weeks in the city, the box is crammed full and everything is semitorn, which is annoying. Don't they think about these things as they stuff, stuff, stuff the envelopes in?

I sit down at one of the gray tables in the Retreat and start sorting things—magazines, a bursar bill, two notes from Mom (one that reads "Happy Spring!" with a baby chick on the cover, and one with a clip from the *Chapel Hill News* about the engagement of two of my high school classmates—weird). There's a postcard from my brother. My parents actually let him go to Cancun with the basketball team for spring break. As if it were like a sports field trip and not an excuse to drink heavily and hook up with girls gone wild. I can barely read his handwriting, but after a few minutes, I work out that it says:

Dear Violet,

I gotta thank you for paving the way to my independence. Cancun f-ing rocks!!!

Your bro,
Jake

I smile. At least he's giving credit where credit is due. Mom and Dad would *never* have let him go on a trip like that if he didn't have the old "You let Violet go model overseas when she was just eighteen" argument in his back pocket.

As I'm walking to the paper-recycling bin to throw away some junk mail and those annoying fall-out subscription cards that were in my magazines, I notice a familiar scrawl wedged in between the pages of *CosmoGirl!*

Violet Greenfield, Box 3389, Vassar College . . .

It's Roger's writing.

I shake out the magazine and let the envelope fall to the ground. I stare at it for a minute, scared to pick it up, as if the piece of paper inside that envelope has the power to break my heart all over again. It must be important, or else he never would have written it down, right?

I pick it up and gather the rest of my mail so I can walk straight to my room. No way can I open the letter in the College Center. In the three minutes that it takes me to get upstairs, I go through roughly a thousand hypotheses about what the letter could say.

It could talk about how he'll be in L.A. this summer, and how he wants me to come with him; it could say that he hates me, that he never wants to see me again; it could say that we're better off just friends, but that he wants our friendship back. Or it could just say, "Have a nice summer." Nah, if it were that, he would have just MySpace-messaged me.

The weird thing is, I don't even know what I *want* it to say, but as I get back to my room, my heart is pounding.

I set my iPod to shuffle and let it pick a letter-reading song. I *need* a good one.

"Gold Digger"—hmm. . . . Not sure how to interpret that.

I tear into the envelope, ripping the top seam so much that I won't be able to replace the letter into the envelope. I hate it when that happens.

V—

Meet me at Dia:Beacon. Noon Sunday.
Please?

R

WTF? A paper letter for that?!

I run down the hall to Kurt's room, where I'm pretty sure I interrupt him and Gregory making out, but they straighten their shirts and act cool. I'm too riled up to feel rude.

"Look at this!" I say, holding the letter out for Kurt.

"Oooh." He looks up at me after he reads it and passes it to Gregory. "A rendezvous!"

"You're missing the point," I say. "Why would he *mail* me something like this?"

"Um, maybe because you wouldn't pick up the phone all week and then you threw him out of Brooklyn," says Gregory.

I glare at Kurt.

"What?" he says, shrugging. "I fill him in on things."

"Whatever," I say. I don't really care what Gregory knows, but I am in full fluster mode about this letter. "The U.S. Postal Service might not have even gotten this to me in time. Did he ever think of that? I mean, we're not living in the age of carrier pigeons and telegrams anymore! How could he be sure I'd even *get* this letter?"

"I think it's romantic," says Kurt. "He left it to fate."

He and Gregory smile at each other. They must be in a major honeymoon phase since they didn't see each other all break.

"I think it's weird and lame," I say, folding my arms over my chest.

"So does that mean you're not going?" asks Kurt.

"No," I say, trying to be coy. "I'm thinking about going."

"Thought so," he says. "Let's pick out an artsy outfit!"

He jumps up and Gregory rolls his eyes.

"One question," I say. "What's the Dia:Beacon?"

"It's a museum, uncultured one," says Gregory, standing up to come with Kurt to my room and help me accessorize.

"Oh," I say sheepishly. "Right. I knew that."

Kurt lets me borrow his car on Sunday to go meet Roger. The Dia:Beacon, I now know, is a museum with modern works from the 1960s on, and it's in an old Nabisco factory. Gregory gave me a lesson in art history as Kurt picked out a Cynthia Vincent shift dress and suede flats for me to wear. "It's librarian chic," said Kurt. My hair is up in a ponytail with a headband in front, because I can't get enough of that style even if it's getting old now. "It's signature," Kurt told me. "Signature looks have no expiration date."

So I feel pretty cute as I put on the bendy metal button they give me to indicate I've paid for entrance. I'm trying not to admit to myself that I dressed up for Roger, but I did. I want him to suffer.

As I walk through the museum, I decide to try to find something by Andy Warhol, the one artist Gregory mentioned whom I'd heard of. But when I start looking around, I feel a chill. It's not just that the space is cold, it's that the art here it is somehow sterile. There's a room that seems empty to me, with wood floors and blank walls, but then I realize there are shapes on the floor, sculptures I guess. I don't think modern art is my thing. I start to miss the Reina Sofia museum in Spain, where I went last year and always had my iPod on the museum playlist so I could hear music while I got cultured.

I'm staring at a bunch of neon light tubes when I feel a tap on my shoulder.

"Hi," says Roger. I feel a rush of warmth.

Although I quickly suppress the smile that automatically comes to my face, I know he saw it.

"Nice place," I say, turning around to walk into the next art-filled (or possibly blank) room.

"I like the garden," Roger says, taking my elbow gently. "Do you want to—?" He points to an exit.

"Yes," I say, relieved that we can leave the warehouse-y interior.

And he's right—the garden is nice. There are cherry trees just blooming and a little wooden boardwalk to stroll on. We walk for a minute or two without saying anything, and then we stop and sit in a set of white plastic chairs.

"I knew you'd like it out here," says Roger.

"It's okay," I say, not really wanting to give him credit for anything.

"I also knew you'd think it was weird of me to ask you to meet me at an art museum," he says. "I know that's not your normal hangout, but I have a paper due on one of the artists shown here anyway, and I thought it would be a unique choice."

"Yeah, well," I say. "I'm thinking of taking art history next year." That's not entirely true, but Gregory mentioned last night that he wants me to because he's appalled at my lack of knowledge. I mean, I'm sort of considering it.

"Really?" says Roger, laughing. "That doesn't seem like you."

"Well, people change, like, all the time," I say, folding my arms and looking away from Roger. "You don't know that much about me, you know."

"Okay, okay," says Roger. "I guess my warm-up banter isn't going well."

I look down at the hangnail next to my thumb. I have an urge to bite it, but I don't want it to start bleeding at an art museum.

"So?" I say curtly. I give him a this-better-be-good look. I know I'm being a brat, but Roger really screwed up.

"Um, well, I guess I wanted to—" he starts. Then he stands up and paces for a minute. I don't think I've ever seen him so agitated.

"Freak," I say. "Sit down. Just say it."

"Well, first," he says, finally pulling it together, "I think Chloe was good for me."

I find myself staring at the hangnail again. *Is this what we're talking about? Chloe?*

"I needed to know that other girls existed," he says. "I mean besides you."

I look up at him but I can't meet his eyes. I stare at his lips as he talks.

"It had been so long, Violet," he says. "You don't even know. Remember when I got you that Valentine's Day card in sixth grade? The one with the squirrel on the front holding a sign that said, 'I'm nuts about you'?"

I smile a little. "Yeah," I say.

"That was this huge confession for me!" he says. "But you just told me it was a bad pun and made me help you analyze the card that Jason Sheridan gave you."

"Jason's card had a skunk on the front," I say. "Remember? It was that French cartoon guy."

"Pepé Le Pew," says Roger. "I know. And I knew that my card didn't matter. That I wasn't on your radar."

"We were friends, Roger," I say. "You never said anything. How was I supposed to—"

"Whatever," Roger says, standing up again and turning away from me. "I don't know why I'm even . . . it doesn't matter now."

He keeps talking, but I can barely hear his voice when the wind starts blowing, so I stand up next to him.

"I'm sorry I messed things up so badly," he's saying. And then he turns to meet my eyes. "Half the time when I was with Chloe, I was thinking about you."

I look down and bite my lip. Part of me loves hearing that, but another part of me feels really sad.

"Thinking about what happened between us makes me feel bad," I say. And when I hear it out loud, I'm surprised I said it. But it's honest.

"Me too," says Roger. "That's not how I wanted it to be."

"Maybe one day it'll matter less," I say, not really to him, but more to myself. It's like a wish I'm sending out into the universe.

We're standing face-to-face, but looking past each other's shoulders, like there's some answer in the distance, or some way to ease the tension if we just don't meet gazes. It feels like forever, and I can't stand it. I can't have things wrong between me and Roger. It's like it throws off the whole world.

I have to forgive him.

"So," I say, wanting to change the subject. Wanting to erase the weirdness and get something—anything—back. "L.A. this summer?"

"Julie told you," he says.

"Yup," I say.

"It should be good," he says, sticking his hands in his pockets and starting to stroll back toward the building. "And you?"

"Home," I say. "I am actually looking forward to hanging out with my parents and Jake. Is that twisted?"

"No," he says. "You haven't been close to home in a while."

"I'll miss you there," I say. It's my peace offering.

Roger looks at me. "You will?" he asks, and I swear I think he's almost tearing up.

"Yeah," I say, looping my arm through his. "You're my best guy friend, after all."

He looks away, but squeezes my arm in close.

We walk out to the parking lot and Roger gives me a big, long hug. When we back away, he says, "It's funny."

"What is?" I ask.

"Oh, nothing," he says, turning to go back inside the museum.

"No—" I say, curious. "What's funny?"

"Seriously, nothing," says Roger. "Friends forever?"

"Only if you spell it with the number four and e-v-a," I say, smiling.

"Deal," he says.

As I pull out of the parking lot, I have the urge to look back.

If he's waiting to watch me drive off, he still loves me, I think.

When I turn my head and look through the rear window, Roger's standing at the entrance, his hand in the air. Like he would have been waving even if I hadn't turned around.

epilogue

    Kurt hung my Gratitude Poster at the foot of my bed, so I'm waking up every morning and remembering all the things I should be happy about. I will never admit that it's kind of working. I've got this Zen-like thing going on with school as I head into the last few weeks of the semester: classes are good, Oliver has started saying hi to me again when we pass each other on campus, and Jess-Fan-Kurt are the best new friends I could hope for.

Even my Sociology class seems to have warmed up to me. In early May, the *Teen Fashionista* profile of me came out, and Miss Mary Janes herself brought it up in class.

"You come across as a three-dimensional model who's a real person," she said. "It's rare."

Then Professor Kirby started talking about how we could all benefit from examining our lives the way I've had to as I navigated the modeling world. This time, I didn't mind being the focus of a class.

Even Angela called and left a message to congratulate me on the article. "Vivacious Violet, you came off marvelously. I am always here for you. Love, Angela." She actually said, "Love, Angela" before she hung up. I haven't called her back yet, but I might, just to avoid a burned bridge. Besides, I got contacted by the Dove people after the story came out—they have such a great campaign about loving yourself, and they want me to somehow be a part of it. So maybe I can be a model *and* follow my own instincts? I'm hoping it's not as impossible as it once seemed.

After all my exams, I'm packing up my room. Julie's driving the Rabbit to Poughkeepsie so we can go home together on a half-the-East-Coast road trip down I-95.

And Roger? We've both been busy, but we're okay. We're IMing, we're e-mailing. And I'm only entertaining my What Might Have Been notions like twice a day. Okay, so I miss him, but I'm determined to enjoy my summer. Maybe it'll be good for me to be alone. Kurt thinks so.

Last night he helped me wrap all my shoes in felt bags so they wouldn't get scuffed. I think he cares about them more than I do. When I gave Kurt a hug good-bye this morning, I almost started crying. Then he said, "Sophomore year is three months away. Please." I'm cheesy but he snapped me out of it.

I'm about to walk out of the front doors of Main dorm when I hear the Rabbit's signature honk. As I roll my two suitcases out to the car, the driver's side door opens.

"Does someone need a ride to Chapel Hill?" Julie smiles as she walks over and takes the handle on one of my bags.

I hoist the other bag into the trunk and walk around to the front seat.

When I pull down the passenger-side mirror to roll on some ChapStick, I see something pop up in the backseat, and I catch my breath.

Roger.

I whip my head around to make sure I'm not just imagining it.

He breaks into a big grin.

I mirror his smile, turning to Julie with a *WTF?* look. My palms are getting all sweaty.

"Well, you know how I hate driving on I-95," says Julie.

"Huh?" I am so confused.

"Roger offered to drive the Rabbit back if I took a flight from New York," she says. "But I told him there was one condition."

"What was that?" I ask, still in surprise mode.

"That I drive *you*, dork!" says Roger, finally speaking and confirming that he is, in fact, in the backseat and that I'm not just having a weird, obsessive hallucination.

"Wait—" I say. "I'm lost. What about L.A.?"

"I opted for the six-week course instead of the twelve," he says. "I needed some time at home. With you."

My heart jumps. But should I be angry? "So you guys arranged this behind my back," I say, folding my arms across my chest.

"I really didn't want to drive, Violet," says Julie. "You know me and that traffic around D.C."

"I asked for a favor," says Roger.

I turn to him and see that his grin is about a mile wide.

"Why?" I ask.

He leans in closer to the front seat, stares at me hard, and says, "It just seems like we should be together this summer."

"What does that mean?" I ask, feeling a little faint.

"I'm not sure," says Roger. "But we have all of I-95 to figure it out."

Make sure your beach bag is packed—grab these awesome
Berkley JAM books!

How I Found the Perfect Dress

BY MARYROSE WOOD

After a summer full of time-travel, Morgan's back to her painfully normal life, until her boyfriend, Colin, presents her with a problem. Faer-
ies are forcing him to boogie with them for eternity, and now she has
to break the spell and save him—all while finding the perfect prom
dress...

The Elite

BY JENNIFER BANASH

When Casey McCloy moves to New York and joins the Upper East
Side's social elite, she couldn't know the drama waiting for her—or the
girl waiting to destroy her rep with one well-timed whisper.

The Guy Next Door

BY CAROL CULVER

Maggie has always been a plain Jane, until the makeover of a lifetime
gives her the tools she needs to make her move on the boy next door—
but will she have the nerve to go for it?

Violet in Private

BY MELISSA WALKER

After global jet-setting and flashing bulbs, Violet thinks she's ready to
give up modeling and concentrate on college. But with Vassar so close
to New York, modeling may not be ready to give up on *her.*

T30.0508